"SUPERB STORYTELLING FROM A WRITER WHO CONTINUES TO FIND A SPECIAL KIND OF MELANCHOLY POETRY IN THE UNFORGIVING LAND- SCAPE OF THE MOUNTAIN STATES."

—BOOKLIST

LET HIM GO

Also by Larry Watson

American Boy
In a Dark Time
Justice
Laura
Leaving Dakota
Montana 1948
Orchard
Sundown, Yellow Moon
White Crosses

LET HIM GO

A Novel

Larry Watson

milkweed
editions

Published 2013 by Milkweed Editions
Printed in Canada
Cover design by Christian Fuenfhausen
Cover image © Ocean/Corbis
Author photo by Susan Watson
20 21 22 23 24   5 4 3 2
First Paperback Edition
ISBN: 978-1-57131-103-0

Milkweed Editions, an independent nonprofit publisher, gratefully acknowledges sustaining support from the Bush Foundation; the Jerome Foundation; the Lindquist & Vennum Foundation; the McKnight Foundation; the National Endowment for the Arts; the Target Foundation; and other generous contributions from foundations, corporations, and individuals. Also, this activity is made possible by the voters of Minnesota through a Minnesota State Arts Board Operating Support grant, thanks to a legislative appropriation from the arts and cultural heritage fund, and a grant from the Wells Fargo Foundation Minnesota. For a full listing of Milkweed Editions supporters, please visit milkweed.org.

Library of Congress Cataloging-in-Publication Data

Watson, Larry, 1947–
    Let him go : a novel / Larry Watson. — First edition.
        pages   cm .
    ISBN 978-1-57131-102-3 (hardcover : alk. paper) — ISBN 978-1-57131-890-9 (e-book)
    1. Grandparent and child—Fiction. 2. Parental relocation (Child custody)—Fiction.
3. Visitation rights (Domestic relations)—Fiction. 4. North Dakota—Fiction. 5. Domestic fiction. I. Title.
    PS3573.A853L48 2013
    813'.54—dc23

                                                                      2013006976

Milkweed Editions is committed to ecological stewardship. We strive to align our book production practices with this principle, and to reduce the impact of our operations in the environment. We are a member of the Green Press Initiative, a nonprofit coalition of publishers, manufacturers, and authors working to protect the world's endangered forests and conserve natural resources. *Let Him Go* was printed on acid-free 100% postconsumer-waste paper by Friesens Corporation.

To Susan

LET HIM GO

1.

September 1951

THE SIREN ON TOP OF THE DALTON, NORTH DAKOTA, fire station howls, as it does five days a week at this hour. Its wail frightens into flight the starlings that roost on the station roof every day yet never learn how fixed and fore-seeable are human lives. The siren tells the town's working citizens and students what they already know. It's twelve o'clock, time for you to fly too. Put down your hammer, your pencil; close your books, cover your typewriter. Go home. Your wives and mothers are opening cans of soup and slicing bread and last night's roast beef for sandwiches. Come back in an hour, ready to put your shoulder to it, to add the figures, parse the sentences, calm the patients, please the customers.

Most drive to their homes, but a man with the width of the town to travel, from Ott's Livestock Sales out on Highway 41 to Teton Avenue in the town's northeast corner, walks. The sun is warm on George Blackledge's back, and he carries his blanket-lined denim coat over his shoulder. But on his way to work that morning in the predawn dark he followed the plumes of his own breath and passed signs of the season's first hard freeze. Blankets and rugs cover-ing the late tomatoes and squash. Windshields needing to be scraped. Thin spirals of smoke rising from chimneys.

Now only in a house or building's western shade or in the shadow of a shed or tree does any white remain. Grass blades and weed stalks that earlier were frost-bent and flattened rise again. Ice skins that grew over gutter pools and alley puddles have melted away. When George enters his house, he notices the lingering smell of hot dust and fuel oil, the stale breath of the furnace that came on during the night for the first time in the season.

But on the kitchen table are not the bowl of tomato soup and the summer sausage sandwich that George has rightly come to expect. Instead on the oilcloth are open cardboard boxes filled with the food that recently has been in their cupboards, bread box, and refrigerator. The house's windows are closed and the curtains drawn, banishing sunlight and, so it seems, sufficient air to breathe.

Into the kitchen comes Margaret Blackledge, about whom people invariably say, Still a handsome woman. Her steel-gray hair is plaited and pinned up. Her chambray shirt is tucked into snug-fitting, faded Levi's. She's wearing boots that have been patched, resoled, and re-heeled so many times they'd rebel at any foot but hers. Those heels make her taller than most women. Draped over one kitchen chair is her wool mackinaw, and on the spindle of another chair her hat hangs by the leather loop that she used to tighten under her chin when she was ready to mount up and ride.

George tilts back his own hat. So this is why you wanted the car today.

You said you didn't mind the exercise.

I don't. But Jesus, Margaret. You really mean to do this?

I do. Margaret Blackledge's eyes have not lost their

power to startle—large, liquid, deep blue, and set in a face whose planes and angles could be sculpted from marble.

With me or without me?

With you or without you. It's your choice. Margaret thrusts her fingers into the back pockets of her jeans and leans against the cupboard. She's waiting, but she doesn't have to say it. She won't wait long.

She nods in the direction of their bedroom. I packed a bag for you, she says. Depending on what you decide.

Nothing fills the silence between them. The Philco on the kitchen counter, which usually squawks livestock prices at this hour, sits mute. The coffeepot whose glass top usually rattles with a percolating fresh brew is emptied, washed, and stored in one of the boxes.

On his way to the bedroom George passes through the living room and he steps over the blankets Margaret has wrapped and tied into tubes to serve as bedrolls.

In the bedroom doorway he pauses, his gaze lingering on both what is there and what is not.

The white chenille bedspread rises over the mound of one pillow but then slopes down to flatness on the other side. The alarm clock ticks on the bedside table. If he stays he'll need reminders of hours and obligations, while she'll be traveling to where time obeys human need and not the other way around. On the top of the bureau the perfume bottle sits, as full as the day she took it out of its gift box. Her brush is gone. So is the framed photograph that often made him pause. His son or his grandson? Did they really look so alike as two-year-olds? Or did they confuse him because they occupied the same space in his heart? Did Margaret even hesitate before she packed the photo? Did she ask herself, Who needs this more, the one who goes or the one who stays?

His suitcase yawns open on the bed, and he walks over to paw through its contents. Clean socks. A few shirts. Two pair of dungarees. Underwear. That old plaid wool railroader's vest. A bandanna. The bottom layers are cold-weather wear—a wool scarf and knit cap, gloves. His sheepskin-lined coat. Long underwear. He leaves the suitcase open and turns back toward the kitchen, a distance that suddenly seems more exhausting than the miles he's already walked today.

In the kitchen he looks over the contents of the boxes. Canned goods, flour, beans—dry and canned—oatmeal, evaporated milk, sugar, coffee, potatoes, apples, carrots. Two cans of Spam and a box of Velveeta. Cups, bowls, plates, forks, knives, and spoons, and that all these are in pairs tells him that she's made all the provisions for him to go. And not much left for him if he decides to stay—she's packed the cast-iron frying pan and the coffeepot, and George Blackledge loves his coffee. A washbasin. Kitchen matches. A can of lard.

What do you mean to cook on? George asks.

Margaret shrugs. An open campfire, if need be. I've got a few camping things set out back. Including that old wire grill you used to set up on rocks over a fire.

With this speech her voice quavers but not with emotion. For years Margaret Blackledge has had a tremor that causes her head to nod and her words to wobble. Harmless, a doctor has called it, but it's unsettling in a woman who seems in every other regard as steady as steel.

George pushes the kitchen window curtain aside. Yes, she's backed their car, an old humpbacked Hudson

Commodore, out of the garage, and a few more supplies for her journey lie in the grass.

You pulled out that old tent, George says. You find the poles and stakes too?

I believe all the pieces are there.

I could set it up, he says. Let the sun burn some of the mildew smell out of the canvas.

I'd just as soon get going.

George walks back over to the chair where her coat and hat wait. He lifts the collar of her mackinaw and rubs the wool between his fingers. I see you've got the long underwear packed too. You planning on being gone right through the winter?

I'm not planning on any length of time. I plan to go, that's all. And stay gone as long as it takes.

What if Lorna says no? George asks. Any mother would.

Margaret says nothing.

You have money?

I went to the bank this morning.

Leave any in there?

A little. Not much.

There wasn't much to begin with.

Margaret's suitcase is waiting by the back door. When she glances in its direction, George feels his eyes smart and his throat tighten.

Think this through, Margaret. What you're aiming to do—

I'll *do*. You ought to know that by now.

What finally made up your mind, if you don't object to my asking?

Not only can I tell you what but when and right down

to the minute. July 27. I know it like it's marked on the calendar. I was coming out of LaVeer's Butcher Shop, and I spied Jimmy over across the street right outside the drugstore. With Donnie and Lorna. In the middle of the day. And neither of them on the job, in spite of their promises and good intentions. Anyway. Jimmy was licking away at an ice cream cone like it was a race whether he or the sun would finish it first. Then he must have licked a little too hard because that scoop of ice cream toppled off the cone. He gave out a little yelp. Donnie saw right away what happened, and so quick the ice cream didn't melt—and this on a day when the sidewalk was hot enough to fry an egg—he reached down and grabbed up that glob of chocolate ice cream. And did he put it back on the cone? He did not. He pushed it right into Jimmy's face. Wait. It gets worse. Then he laughed. Donnie *laughed*. By this time Jimmy's wailing like his little heart is breaking. And what do you suppose Lorna did? Pick him up and wipe his face and his tears like any mother would? She did not. She kept right on walking. And she was wearing a smile, George. A *smile*. To do a child that way? A child that bears my son's name? It was all I could do not to cross the street and snatch that little boy and run like hell. But I had my pork chops damn near cooking in my arms, and I suppose I was hearing your cautions so I continued on my way. But I knew, George; I *knew. That boy did not belong with those people.* So even with all you said—it's wrong, it's useless, it might even be against the law—my mind was made up. It wasn't more than a week later when I got my resolve screwed down tight, and I went to that little basement apartment they'd been renting. But they were gone. Bound for Montana, I learned. And owing three months' rent. So because I held my tongue on that July day they got a couple months' head start. But I'm heading out now, George, and you have to choose. Go or stay. But decide. Now.

I have to piss.

In the bathroom the matching towels and washcloth are no longer hanging on the rack. Only a threadbare towel is suspended from the bar over the tub—his to use in her absence. This morning's sliver of soap is no longer stuck to the sink's porcelain. In the medicine cabinet only George's shaving supplies still rest on the shelf, but his empty toilet kit waits open-mouthed on the tub for his razor, shaving cream, toothbrush, and aspirin.

Her things might be packed up but the room's very air remains hers. The smell of her shampoo, her cold cream. The steam that rose from her bathwater. And then from her as she stepped dripping from the tub. Could he ever stop breathing these, no matter how long she'd been gone?

He stands over the toilet. If there is a moment, an instant, when George Blackledge isn't sure what he'll do, by the time he's opened his trousers and pulled out his cock, that moment has passed. He sighs, the deep breath and exhalation of a man about to follow someone onto a narrow ledge. Such a man is often cautioned not to look down. He might well be advised not to look forward or backward either.

Back in the kitchen he asks, Did you call Janie? Does she know about this plan of yours?

I mailed her a letter this morning.

You don't even give your daughter a chance to talk you out of this?

She has no say in this. None. But I told her you'd let her know if you decide to stay home.

Did you gas up the car?

I thought I'd do that on the way out of town.

Why don't I do it now? I need to swing by Ott's and give Barlow the word.

I don't suppose he'll be too happy.

You can be damn sure of that. I leave now, that's probably over for good.

I'm sorry.

But not sorry enough to cast this goddamn idea of yours aside.

Margaret reaches under the sink and brings out a can of Ajax. When she shakes its powder into the sink, a chalky ammoniac odor fills the room. If you're coming with me, George, that'll have to be the end of it. No dragging your heels. No second-guessing. No what ifs. If you're with me, you're with me.

She turns back to the sink and begins to scour its porcelain. Soon she's scrubbing so hard even her ass is in motion. Nothing but two hard mounds of muscle and fat bunching under denim faded almost to white. No, there was never any doubt what George would do.

Should I shut off the water? he asks.

Might as well. We don't want to come home to busted pipes.

2.

AROUND THE CORNER FROM THE MOBIL STATION IS Oscar's Roundup Bar and Lounge, On and Off Sale, a dimly lit establishment barely wide enough for a bar and row of booths. When George enters, the only customer is Elmer Will, sitting at the end of the bar and pulling on a bottle of Schlitz in between spoonfuls of chili. Walking through a single shaft of dusty sunlight, George makes his way down the bar to where Randy Pettig is jamming a towel into a high-ball glass. At the sight of George Blackledge, Randy smiles, raises his hands, and says, Don't shoot. I'll come peaceable.

You didn't then, George says. Why would you now? He points toward a row of bottles. A pint of Four Roses.

Randy drops his hands. Four Roses it is, he says, his voice flattened with disappointment. He finds the bourbon, drops it into a bag, and twists the paper around the bottle's neck. As he's ringing up the sale he tries once more. It's been a while, he says to George.

And it will be again, George replies.

. . .

Margaret carries the box of canned goods outside and sets it down next to the driveway, convenient and quick to pack into the car when George returns. Before she can cross the yard and return to the house, however, a plump young woman in a print dress and an apron hurries out of the house next door.

The woman waves exuberantly to Margaret. Hello, she calls out.

Good afternoon.

Having a rummage sale, are you?

No, says Margaret.

I seen the boxes and I thought maybe . . . She smiles. An upper tooth is missing, and her lip snags on that open space. Even so, it's a nice smile, wide and unsullied. She puts her hands in the pockets of her apron and says, Eddie's got me on a pretty tight allowance so I'm always on the lookout for a bargain.

Sorry, replies Margaret. Can't help you.

Taking a trip, then?

Could be.

No boundary markers separate the yards. The sun at its midday height sheds light and heat equally on each side. Nothing distinguishes one property from another, unless it's grass a fraction of an inch higher on one side or a sweeter green on the other. Yet something keeps a distance between these two women as surely as a fence so tall it would have to be shouted over.

You want us to keep an eye on things? the young woman asks. Bring in your mail or your paper?

Won't be necessary, Margaret says. If you'll excuse me now . . .

The plump young woman remains in place, her hands kneading the interiors of her apron pockets. Can I ask you something?

Margaret stops but she's one of those people whose body can convey impatience even in repose.

When my husband comes home, the young woman says, he'll ask me what I did today. And I'll tell him I talked to the lady next door. After all these years, Eddie will say, And she's still the lady next door? What's her *name*, Mary?

Margaret has to know what the woman wants but instead she says, Three years. Not all that many. And Margaret continues on her way. Before she reaches her back door, however, she turns back to her neighbor. Margaret Blackledge. Perhaps because she has pronounced that name so many times over the years, she can say it without her voice's usual warble.

Mary Bremmer, the young woman says, then adds, Pleased to meet you, but Margaret's door has already closed behind her.

Mary Bremmer has barely had time to shut her own door—to shut her door and bite off a few squares of a Hershey bar—when the front doorbell chimes. Mary hurries to answer it.

Standing on the porch is the woman who now has a name. Margaret Blackledge thrusts out her tanned, rough hand. In case some chocolate might be on her fingers, Mary Bremmer wipes her hand quickly on her apron before taking Margaret's hand.

I want to do this proper, says Margaret. And that means walking right up to your front door and apologizing for my bad manners. For my *years* of bad manners.

That's all right, Mary says, chocolate melting between her tongue and the roof of her mouth.

No. No, it's not all right. I've been a poor excuse for a

neighbor. And I don't have a single good reason for my behavior. I just thought . . . I'm not sure what I thought. That we wouldn't be here in Dalton all that long so it would be best not to form attachments.

But now, Mary says, you're going, and she pulls her hand free from Margaret's.

That I am, says Margaret. So this is the day I finally say pleased to meet you and good-bye.

Good-bye.

And as Margaret Blackledge backs away, Mary Bremmer gives her neighbor a tiny wave before closing her door. Her hand hovers in the air as if she's about to throw the bolt, but then she stops. The middle of the day—why would anyone need to lock a door?

. . .

The bourbon's fumes scald his nostrils but its burn is a comfort in his chest and belly. He could have used that heat as he walked to work this morning. He shudders and screws the cap back on. He says softly, Enough, a man more comfortable making promises to himself than to others. When he reaches under the front seat of the Hudson to hide the bottle, his hand lands on another package, something wrapped in one of the terry cloth towels that hung in the bathroom this morning. The shape and heft of this parcel, its location—what else could it be? But George brings it out and unwraps it anyway. Yes. What else could it be. The .45 automatic that the United States Army issued to George Blackledge during the First World War. He ejects the clip. Empty. He works the pistol's action to make sure a round isn't chambered. He wraps it up again and drops its unmistakable weight on the passenger seat.

He feels again under the seat and finds a box of cartridges.

. . .

Margaret replaces the lid on the garbage can, and at the sound of the Hudson's tires on the gravel driveway she stops and waits for George, one hand on her hip and the other shading her eyes as though she's watching him approach from a distance.

If she notices that he's getting out of the car with her blue terry cloth towel wadded in his hand, she doesn't mention it. She smiles and asks, Do you want those leftover potatoes or should I throw them out?

For answer George grabs her above the elbow, but he's not just squeezing her arm, he's pushing too, guiding her across the grass and toward the back door. It's a day for firsts. The first frost of the season. The first drink he's taken in eleven years. The first time he's laid a hand on his wife in anger, much less touched her with a weapon in his other hand.

In the kitchen he lets her go as roughly as he grabbed her, then drops the towel-wrapped gun on the table. Its muffled thud is like nothing ever heard within these walls.

What the hell, Margaret. What the *hell*.

She has backed up across the kitchen. Her upper chest and throat are blotchy, and the blood keeps rising, up past the hard, sharp angle of her jaw to those sculpted cheekbones and across that high forehead. Because Margaret

Blackledge doesn't embarrass easily, that color can only be the color of anger, and soon her suntanned face is the shade of cinnamon.

That wasn't for you to find, she says. I put that there before I knew you'd be coming with me.

But you thought you'd need it?

I didn't want to find I did and then not have it.

Jesus, Margaret.

You've heard the stories about Donnie.

Talk. Just talk. And you know what that counts for. George flips back a corner of the towel, exposing an inch of blue-black barrel. Was this going to be part of your argument?

You don't know me any better than to ask that?

And you bought a box of cartridges?

She says nothing but stares hard at her husband. She presses a palm to her jaw, though any attempt to stop the vibration is useless. Put it back, George. Put it back. And then you stay. You've got no heart for any of this, anyway.

He takes a deep breath, exhales, then tilts his head back and breathes again as though the oxygen he needs were at a height he can't quite reach. Closed up like this the house can't take in the sun's heat, and whiskey won't help with the chill of an empty house. George refolds the towel, then picks up the bundle.

I'll pack the tent, he says. Mildew smell and all.

3.

BEFORE GEORGE HAS EVEN TURNED OFF THE IGNITION, Barlow Ott has exited the trailer that serves as the temporary office for Ott's Livestock Sales. The car's engine shudders, clunks to silence, and George opens his door to greet Barlow as he lugs his heavy-gutted body toward the Hudson.

Margaret leans across the seat to advise her husband, Don't let him shame you.

Peering into the back window, Barlow sees the boxes of supplies stacked in the backseat. Well, hell. Of course you're not coming back to work this afternoon if you're moving. Sell your house over the noon hour, did you?

George steps out of the car. We've got family business that needs attending to, Barlow.

Ott grooms the wings of his thick moustache with the knuckle of his index finger, bends down, then touches the brim of his hat. Howdy, Margaret. Running off with one of my best hands, are you?

Hello, Barlow. I'll bring him back to you good as new.

Ott stands stiffly. At his nod, George follows him toward the trailer, its white aluminum siding glaring in the afternoon sunlight.

Barlow asks, Is this because you're not working with the horses?

Family business. Like I said.

It's no reflection, Ott says. I put a man where I need him.

George's back is still knotted tight from spending the morning working on the new office building. He held the sheetrock in place while a man a third his age hammered the nails.

Because if it's the difference between you staying or going, Ott says, I could maybe shift things around and have you working stock.

I hired on here for wages. Not because I need to pat a horse now and then.

Barlow Ott squints as if he were staring into the sun. But he's only gazing up through the head-and-a-half distance between his eyes and George's stone-blue ones.

Jesus, Ott says. Does it ever occur to you to do things the easy way? A man's willing to do you a favor . . .

George glances back at his wife waiting in the Hudson. Speaking of paychecks.

Right. Barlow Ott starts up the stairs to the trailer office. He leans hard on the handrail as if he needs to haul his body up the steps. Before he goes inside, he turns back to George Blackledge. Friday was payday so it won't be much.

I know what I've got coming. And if you've got it in cash, that would save me a trip back into town.

George turns his back on the trailer as if any business done there did not bear witnessing. Back in the car, Margaret is craning her head out the window and looking skyward. Overhead a hawk has found a thermal to ride, and its tilting, silent-winged body is the only moving thing between the bright sun and the shadowless dust below.

The trailer's door rattles open. Barlow Ott stands at the top of the steps and holds a few bills down to George, who takes them without counting and puts them into a wallet whose black leather has worn and frayed to gray at the fold and corners.

Little extra there, Ott says, because it's the last.

Appreciate it.

Because it's the last.

You need a receipt because it's cash?

The last. You understand what I'm saying? Like severance pay. You're a damn good worker, George. You show up sober every day and on time. You do what you're told and you don't waste time leaning on your shovel. But I took you on as a favor. You don't want the work, there's plenty of strong young backs out there waiting to take your place. I can't hold the job for you.

As George listens to Barlow Ott's lecture, the knots of his jaw work so hard and fast it seems as though he'll swallow anything he has to say. But he gets the words out. I understand, Barlow. Then George holds his wallet aloft. And like I say, I appreciate it.

He turns and starts toward the car, shoving his wallet back into his pocket where a faded rectangle in the denim has been waiting for the billfold's return.

To George's back Barlow says, But tell that wife of yours I can always use a little extra help with the books.

Over his shoulder George replies, *She'd* need to work

with the horses, but enough wind blows between the two men that those words might not have arrived at their destination.

Once he's back in the car George reports none of his conversation, so it's left to Margaret to say, I couldn't hear what the two of you were talking about, but it didn't look all that cordial. Is there something between you and Barlow I don't know about?

George turns the key in the ignition and pulls down hard on the shift lever. As if he's trying not to raise any dust, he drives slowly away from the trailer. I once ran in Barlow's kid brother.

Franklin? For good cause, I assume.

He was using his wife as a punching bag. So yes, I'd say.

What was Barlow's position? Let me guess: she had it coming.

Something like that.

You never told me about that. Arresting Franklin, I mean.

Didn't I.

But then I'm sure there were plenty of arrests you never told me about.

Not much to most. I guess I brought home those that had some excitement to them.

Or if I knew the principals?

Hell, you probably knew them all. I never had much in the way of out-of-town business.

They drive past a young man stripped down to his undershirt, and though his battered straw hat is pulled down to his eyebrows, George sees enough of his face to raise a finger in greeting. The young man waves back with a hammer that George also recognizes.

I went to school with Franklin, Margaret says. As a matter of fact, he took me to a county dance or two.

He mentioned at the time he was once one of your suitors.

You remember that? After all these years?

You'd be surprised what sticks, considering how much that doesn't.

Franklin was probably trying to appeal to your sentimental side.

That worked a time or two.

But not for Franklin.

Not after I saw his wife.

Yet with that between you two, Barlow hired you.

That he did.

Once the Hudson's tires touch the highway's asphalt, George stomps down hard on the accelerator. Now let's see, George says, how long it takes to get the smell of horseshit out of my nose.

4.

EVENTUALLY THE HIGHWAY THE BLACKLEDGES TRAVEL
will lead through the fiery eruptions of rock that are the
Dakota Badlands—mile after mile of jagged, sheered-off red
and orange buttes and sudden deep-shadowed gorges and
ravines—but the first few miles out of Dalton are as easy as a
pony ride. This is prairie, rolling gentle country where black
seams of trees and brush stitch one grassy hill to another.
Barbed wire lines the highway, but with so much emptiness
on every side, what the wire is supposed to fence in or out
isn't clear. Here and there an unmarked dirt or gravel path
branches off from the highway, leading no doubt to a ranch
or farm, but these are far enough from the main road that it
would take a soaring hawk's eye to find them. At one of the
breaks in the wire—was a gate here once?—a turnoff barely
as wide as a car appears, and George shifts down to second
and turns the car hard off the highway, swerving so suddenly
it seems as though he must be trying to avoid a collision.

A box on the backseat slides against the door, and cans
and jars crash into each other. Margaret is pitched hard
against her own door, but she rights herself quickly and
reaches toward the steering wheel as if she means to take
control of the car.

Don't, George! Don't do this!

But George pushes her hand away and concentrates on maneuvering the car up the narrow road, its soft dirt almost as difficult to negotiate as drifted snow. The dust the Hudson raises finds its way through George's open window, and he risks taking a hand off the wheel for the time it takes to roll up the window.

Margaret slumps back in her seat, powerless now to prevent her husband from taking them where he's decided they'll go.

At the hill's crest the road bends around a stand of bur oak before briefly widening and leveling out. Here George stops. If he didn't, they'd drive a curving route down the other side of the hill. The road eventually stops at a ranch huddled in the valley below.

I don't need to see this again, says Margaret, swatting her hand in the direction of a white frame house, a windmill, a small corral, and a barn and stable, their wood weathered to the color of a sparrow's feathers. Although the valley and a few cottonwoods shelter the ranch house and its outbuildings, every wall and fence post seems wind-worn and leaning, nothing quite plumb, square, or true, everything down there as temporary as a season.

Because you remember it like this?

What it is. What it was. Margaret looks at her husband. Did you think I could ever forget it?

You'd be better off if you did.

Might as well say I'd be better off not drawing breath.

We're talking about a *place*, Margaret. Boards. Nails. A few blades of grass and a hell of a lot of dirt in between. Eight hundred acres that never promised or delivered anything but hardship.

She rolls her window all the way down and hangs her head out as if she's going to be sick. When she draws back inside she says, Don't tell me what it is.

She'd protested coming here as urgently as if she'd been in mortal danger, but now Margaret Blackledge stares down into that valley so steadily her tremor seems to subside.

If he were not beside but behind her, George might be able to align his vision with hers, like sighting a rifle, and determine exactly the target of her gaze. The possibilities seem to be few. Give the mind the opportunity to work its memory magic, however, and absences can be as evocative as presences. And this man and woman have reached the age at which they are as likely to see what's not there as what is . . . the circle where the horse tank once was, the grass blades still furled after decades of being matted down. The indentation in the earth where the homestead's original sod house stood, but there the grass grows two shades greener for once having had the concentration of lives lived within its rectangle. The bare space beyond the back door where the lilacs grew and gave the twins shade for their play and Margaret her smell of spring when she needed it most.

George once woke in the night and stood at the kitchen window, water glass in hand, and looking out saw a face, someone standing among the lilacs and watching the house.

Without turning on a light, grabbing a weapon or a robe, or putting something on his feet, George burst from the house and ran like a man heedless of danger and certain of the identity of the person hiding in the shrubbery.

Well short of the confrontation he appeared eager for, George stopped.

Margaret had given the children a few old dishes, and

under the bower of the lilacs they would dig holes and fill the cracked, chipped cups, bowls, and plates with what they scooped from the earth. But there must have been something besides digging to the children's make-believe because they had balanced plates in the lilacs' branches. It was one of those that had caught enough moonlight to look like a face, pale and yearning and turned toward the Blackledge home.

The night was cold and his bed was waiting, but George remained in place, staring into the mesh of interlaced bare branches, the season for blossom and fragrance long past. And when the ranch's sale was final and the Blackledges were moving out, it was Margaret who insisted the lilacs be chopped down. We can't do that, George argued. They'd bought those as sure as the house and the barn and the land they were built on. And burn the branches, was her answer.

Now no sign, no scorch or char, marks the place where George built the fire. Remarkable, earth's strength to re-store itself and erase human effort. But memory, stronger still, can send flames as high as the roof, and shift the wind and choke George and sting his eyes with smoke, lilac smoke, as though it could be differentiated from any other.

Margaret too is looking down less on a place than on a time . . . when everything—house, barn, corral, lilacs, good grass, and winding creek—was in its place yet none were visible.

The first landmark to vanish was the hill they sit on now, as the snowstorm rolled down the eastern slopes of the Rockies, picked up speed as it crossed Montana, and everywhere in its wake left a featureless landscape, both distance and contours of earth erased. The windows of the Blackledges' house hummed and rattled in their frames, snow hissed against the outer walls, and wind whistled down the chimney. Her house was blizzard-besieged, but Margaret had her hands full with the people inside. Some kind of bug had bitten George and the twins, and all of them were sick, going off like Roman candles at both ends, vomiting in kitchen pots and scurrying to the toilet with diarrhea. George bore his illness with nothing but groans, but James and Janie called for Margaret with every cramp and convulsion. Between times when she was holding someone over the toilet or changing bedding, Margaret would glance out at the storm. And be glad. Their illnesses had come on during the night, and they all woke that morning unable to climb out of bed except to scramble to the bathroom. That meant that the twins didn't go off to school, and George didn't drive into town or ride off to mend a fence or feed stock. She didn't have to worry about any or all of them finding their way home through the storm. She and George had installed indoor plumbing two years before, so that problem was solved. The wind could howl and the snow drift high: Margaret Blackledge had her children and her husband safe—sick but safe—in rooms she could oversee. She'd have been a fool to ask for more from this life.

Margaret extends her arm out the car window and marks an *X* in the air. It's close to the gesture a priest makes, but if she were to speak, her benediction might be nothing but her father's original homestead claim. The southeast quarter of section 14, township 132, range 99, Dalton County,

North Dakota. In Margaret's memory those numbers are as fixed as any dates drilled into the minds of schoolchildren.

She brings her hand back in and touches it to her long, slender throat. She continues to look outward but now it's to her husband she speaks. I've had enough loss, George.

You know that's what life is. Loss, fast or slow. Jesus, if the years teach us anything—

That doesn't mean I have to sit back and take it. Not while I have strength or will to do something.

Accept it or not. Nothing lasts. He slaps his hand against the Hudson's dashboard. Not flesh or steel. Not walls or possessions. Not friends or family. Hell, look around. This is the country of all that *isn't* anymore. You don't need me to make a list.

You're right, George. Her eyes flash like sunlight on window glass. I don't need a goddamn list. And I didn't need a trip out here as a goddamn reminder of anything.

But a list like that, once its enumeration has begun, has its own momentum. Comfort, but pain too. Certainty, but doubt too. Strength. Beauty. Desire. Love. And one day only the memory of all those . . . and then not even memory.

George wrestles the gearshift into reverse and executes the turn that will take them back to the highway. It's a road they've driven thousands of times before but which they both believed they'd never travel again.

5.

DRIVING WEST AND NORTH OUT OF DALTON, GEORGE and Margaret listen to the quiz show *Winner Take All* on the Dickinson radio station, though neither of them is able to answer a single question. When they lose this program to static, Margaret twists the dial back and forth until she finds a program out of Glasgow, a swap shop that comes in as clear as a meadowlark's call. They shake their heads over the caller who has a pair of salt and pepper shakers for sale—fully loaded, he says—and they smile at the caller who wants to buy a scythe because his grass got away from him over the summer. Then those voices fade and are replaced by a crackle and hiss that sounds as though someone recorded blowing sand.

In the absence of other voices, Margaret says, Maybe you're worried he'd grow up spoiled if he lived with us.

A straight, level stretch of highway. No other cars on the road. But George Blackledge says nothing and stares out the windshield as if the world out there were asking for all his attention.

Maybe you think, Margaret continues, I couldn't bring myself to discipline him. And we know you wouldn't. That's something I could never figure out about you, George. You could stand up to a mad-dog drunk and haul him off to the hoosegow but you couldn't speak a cross word to your children. But come to me about it—oh, that was easy enough for you. James has to break the ice on the horse tank first thing, not when it suits him. Janie's dawdling when she's gathering eggs again. So then it was my job to get after them. I used to wonder if that's when the tremors started, when I had to hand out my own scoldings and yours too. I'd be mad as hell at you for giving me that duty but I had to turn it around on the twins. Not fair, George. It wasn't fair.

As intently as he stares straight ahead, she stares at him, at that large skull that must be filled with words—*it must be*—but which remains as silent as if it were chiseled from granite. She waits a mile or more, until the road finds a reason to curve, a grassy butte hardly high enough to justify going around. I give up, Margaret says. Again.

She tries the radio dial once more, and soon she finds a Williston station where an announcer tells them they're listening to *The Northern Plains Gospel Hour.* But before so much as a line of a song is out—*I'm just a poor*—George reaches over and snaps off the radio.

Goodness, says Margaret.

I try to stay out of their churches, George says. They can keep their goddamn music out of my car.

That would make it my fault, Margaret says, for inviting it in. But it's just a song, George. A pretty song. You've probably heard me sing it myself. Though the way I massacre a tune, you maybe wouldn't recognize it.

Then turn it back on if you like, George says. He takes out his pack of Lucky Strikes, shakes one loose, and brings it to his lips. Without being asked, Margaret pushes in the cigarette lighter.

That's not what I'm saying. But when it comes to letting things go, George Blackledge, you sure as hell talk a better game than you play. How many years ago did you walk away from your father? And you're still looking over your shoulder. Just because he was a Bible-thumper—

And if it was just Bibles he thumped, that'd be a different story.

Fine. A man who beat his wife and children. A cruel man.

The lighter pops out and he brings its glowing rings to the tip of his cigarette. He inhales deeply and then blows a stream of smoke toward the small window vent. And a tyrant, says George. A cruel tyrant.

All right. He was all you say and then some. But my God, the man's been dead and gone for how many years? And you still can't listen to a hymn? It must have been hell for you, sitting through James's service.

Like it was for you. And the music didn't have a goddamn thing to do with it.

Now it is George who turns the radio back on.

I'm just a-going over Jordan. I'm just a-going over—

And it's Margaret who turns it off.

The sun has dropped low enough to bring up the colors in the prairie grasses, the shades of lavender and gold that can't be seen at any other moment of the day and that incline most travelers through this landscape to silence. Gospel hour indeed.

6.

WHEN THEY ARRIVE IN BENTROCK, THE COUNTY SEAT
of Mercer County, Montana, dusk has finally let loose its
long hold on the day. Darkness has fallen from the apex of
the sky and risen from the rooftops and tall trees, taking
over all but a streak of the western horizon. Streetlamps
and porch lights have come on and windows have been
closed against the evening chill. The only birds flying at
this hour are the nightjars hunting insects stirred by the
day's heat. The owls are waiting for that blood-red smear
in the west to disappear.

To drive into this little town from the wide, undulat-
ing, horizontal world of the prairie means to experience an
abrupt alteration of scale. Here people have tried to in-
stall the vertical, though they've been modest about it. No
building rises higher than two stories. The trees have had
less than a century to grow. A water tower, a few church
steeples, a grain bin, the cupola on the courthouse—these
are darker forms against the backdrop of the night.

Because this town is small and all its intentions apparent, even to a first-time visitor, the Blackledges have
no difficulty finding Main Street and the hotel where they
plan to spend the night. Even easier to locate is the nearby
courthouse, a brick and stone structure that also houses

the county jail and the sheriff's office. The entrance to both is at the back of the building, and George pulls in to the unpaved lot and parks the car.

I want to see if Sheriff Hayden's in, George says. He and I worked on an extradition case once. Knew a hell of a lot more law than I did. When we explain our situation, I believe he'll be able to provide some direction.

As her husband opens the car door, Margaret asks, Isn't it late for him to be here?

The light's on. And they don't keep bankers' hours. You of all people ought to know that.

Fine. But don't tell him more than you need to.

I couldn't if I wanted to.

What I mean is, this isn't a legal matter.

No, George says, stepping out of the car. Not so far it isn't.

Margaret climbs out too. My God. How can I get this sore doing nothing but sitting in a car? You go ahead, she says, first reaching high overhead and then bending down to touch her toes. I'll stay out here and stretch my legs and enjoy the evening air.

George heads toward the jail, and Margaret proceeds in the other direction, striding across the gravel with the long-legged pace of someone measuring off distance. When she reaches the farthest corner of the lot, she stops, wraps her arms around herself as protection against the dropping temperature, and sniffs the air. Although she can't see it from here, just down the block from the courthouse is a greenhouse. She and George commented on it as they drove past, its glass walls and roof reflecting light from a sky that to their eyes held nothing but darkness. And inside would be other elements rapidly vanishing from the outer autumnal world—warmth, soft dirt, fragrances from flowers blossoming according to their own season. What must it be like, on a night like this, when another hard freeze is coming on, or during a winter snow, to smell moist dirt and what grows from it, when even the odor of decay is welcome . . . She looks up at the sky where, within the hour, the first stars have appeared. Long past the moment when her neck begins to stiffen and ache, she continues to stare into the darkness, even though none of the human secrets she needs to know are to be found in the stars but rather closer to the earth her boots stand upon.

Finally she walks back to the car. She doesn't get inside but leans against the hood and its still-warm metal. Soon she hears footsteps kicking through the gravel, and in the light from the jail's back door she sees two men approaching. They might be doubles, a pair of tall, slow-moving men who walk as though they have yokes across their broad shoulders, yet something in their carriage hints that they can carry still more weight. They're wearing uniforms issued by the same army—sweat-rimmed Stetsons, plaid shirts with snaps instead of buttons, Levi's, and boots. The man who is not Margaret's husband takes off his hat as he comes near.

Margaret, George says, this is Jack Nevelsen. Jack's sheriff here. Wes Hayden's been out of office for some time now.

With the two men standing side by side, it's apparent that George Blackledge has years on Jack Nevelsen, but the resemblance is close enough for them to be father and son. Does being sheriff give a man that distant, careworn look, or will people in this part of the world elect only a man who has it?

Pleased to meet you, ma'am, Nevelsen says, extending his hand. Yes, the Haydens are living in Fargo now. Wes and his family, anyway.

I explained our situation, George says.

Nevelsen nods and though there's no light overhead but what comes from the stars, when he puts his hat back on his eyes are cast deeper in darkness. The thing is, Nevelsen says, the Weboy clan has two branches. Like I told your husband, the ones up here—they're townsfolk. Good people. They've had a little hard luck but they're hardworking and law-abiding. Frontier Saddlery here, that's a Weboy operation. Or at least started up by the family. But from what I've heard, the Weboys down around Gladstone are nothing but trouble. Always looking for the easy dollar and not much caring how they get it. That's the branch Donnie's from, and maybe that's where you'd find him. Back with his people. If he'd landed anywhere around here, especially with a young woman and a child, I'd have heard.

Margaret turns a slow circle as if to verify her location. Donnie talked about living up here. I'm sure of that.

Yes ma'am. He spent a few summers here. Staying with his aunt and uncle. On the run maybe, though Sheriff Hayden would have been the one to know for sure about that. Nothing but rumor ever came across my desk about Donnie. You say he's married to the woman? And they've got a little boy?

The boy's a Blackledge, Margaret is quick to say. His mother was married to our son.

Jack Nevelsen nods. All right, I have it. His voice drops to an even gentler register. Your grandson.

Our grandson. The sternness that jumped into Margaret's voice a moment ago is gone too.

If we could ask one more favor, George says. We were planning to put up at the Northern Pacific Hotel. Is that our best bet here?

Jack Nevelsen takes his hat off and slaps it lightly against his thigh like a man embarrassed by his own clumsiness. Nora's folks are here, he says, otherwise we could put you up. But sure. The Northern Pacific's fine. A damn sight better than the Wagon Wheel, out on the west edge of town. The hotel's run-down a bit from what it once was, but it's clean and mostly quiet.

Clean is all I need, Margaret says. Thank you again.

All three shake hands once more, the sign that their transactions are concluded.

But no. Before the Blackledges can get back into their car, Sheriff Nevelsen stops them. Wait up. Here's a thought. I've got an empty jail here. Not a prisoner in it. Four cells with cots, and you're welcome to bunk down here. It's as clean as the hotel and even quieter. And a hell of a lot cheaper. With your former line of work being what it was, I figure it wouldn't bother you. And I don't know about Mrs. Blackledge, but my Nora's been in and out of that jail so often it's like another room of our house.

Margaret holds up her hand in gratitude. Thank you for your offer, Mr. Nevelsen. We'll take you up on it. I don't have any prejudices or superstitions that would keep me from spending a night in your accommodations. A night in jail! I never thought it would come to that!

If any of the residents in any of the small, watchful houses across the street hear Margaret, would they recognize the sound of a woman laughing? On this street?

On this chilly autumn night? They'd be more likely to believe they were hearing a swift stream rushing over stones, though they're far from any water that moves faster than a slow walk.

And you said the magic word, Margaret adds. Clean.

7.

SHERIFF NEVELSEN ENCOURAGES THE BLACKLEDGES TO take the two cells with the best mattresses, which will mean that George and Margaret will not spend the night next to each other. Margaret accedes to this arrangement, and George insists that she take the larger cell, though when it comes right down to it, neither is more than a narrow room bare but for an iron cot and a small shelf built right into the wall. Since neither barred door will be locked and George and Margaret will have access to a toilet, Sheriff Nevelsen removes the slop bucket from each cell.

Sheriff Nevelsen hands a small stack of sheets and towels to Margaret. For what it's worth, he says, the towels are from our place. Not jail-issue. The sheets—Nora uses nothing but hot water, and she's generous with the bleach. Sorry I haven't got something better in the way of blankets. And I thought I had some pillows somewhere, but damned if I can find them now.

These will do just fine, says Margaret. You didn't have to go to all this trouble.

We have some bedding in the car, George adds. We packed for the long haul.

Margaret flaps open a sheet over the bare mattress. Yes,

the smell of bleach flutters through the cell and perhaps even a faint scent of the sunlight that dried the sheets.

Sheriff Nevelsen leans in the open door and takes out his cigarettes. He offers the pack to George and Margaret and when they refuse, he lights one for himself. Who's working the ranch in your absence? he asks.

Margaret glances over at her husband as if she hopes he'll be the one to answer this question. When it's plain that George doesn't intend to speak, she says, We sold the ranch a few years back.

But you were doing both, Nevelsen asks, law enforcement and running the ranch?

So to speak, George replies. It was mostly Margaret kept it going. If it had been me alone working the place, even if I could have done it full-time, we'd have gone under long ago.

Don't listen to him, Mr. Nevelsen, Margaret says. For years he was working more hours than there were in a day and doing a damn good job at everything he turned his hand to.

Running for sheriff, George says, was supposed to come second to running the ranch. I thought a regular paycheck from the county would give us a little breathing room.

Jack Nevelsen blows a stream of smoke toward the jail cell's low ceiling. I can imagine how well that worked.

I don't have to tell you, says George, law enforcement will take all you can give it and still ask for more.

Same as ranching, says Margaret.

George nods in agreement. Same as ranching. It was Margaret's to work or lease or sell. Her people homesteaded that land. And she was her father's top hand almost from the day she could sit on a horse.

Margaret says, We made it work for a good many years. Damn near wore George down to the nub but we kept it going. But after our son died, we had his wife and son living with us. It was mostly for them we sold and moved to town. Thought she'd be better off with the company of people her own age.

And that turned out to be Donnie Weboy, interjects Jack Nevelsen.

That was Donnie. So you can see how that came back on us. But it was for the boy too. He could be closer to school, when the time came.

George shakes a Lucky Strike out of his pack, scratches a match on the rough wall, and lights his own cigarette. She makes it sound all personal, he says. Our circumstances weren't so far off from a hell of a lot of folks'. We had a run of hard years. The price of cattle kept going down. One drought year after another. I tried a little wheat farming and no sooner got started than we got hailed out.

Sheriff Nevelsen says, It's a wonder how anyone with a small spread makes a go of it in this part of the country.

But some do, says George. When we finally sold, it felt like . . . I don't know—

Oh, hell, says Margaret. It was time. Past time.

The cell door does not swing open or closed but slides on a steel track, and now Jack Nevelsen moves the door a few inches in one direction and then the other. How'd your boy die, if you don't mind my asking?

George and Margaret exchange the look that so often passes between husbands and wives: *Are you going to tell this or am I?*

But was there ever any doubt?

Margaret Blackledge sits down on the cot before she

begins. She braces her chin in her hand as if she knows that telling this story will bring more than the usual vibration to her voice.

Thrown from a horse, of all things, and this was a boy who practically grew up in the saddle. Who was happier in the company of horses than of children his own age. And who loved saddles and tack the way some boys loved their toy soldiers. James kept hoping something would change so he could come back to the ranch for good, but that hadn't worked out. So he was driving a truck for a local fuel oil company, and he and Lorna and their little boy were living in town. But they visited often enough and on this particular day, early August it was, they'd come out for a home-cooked Sunday supper. After, while we were all sitting outside digesting our meal, James decided he'd ride the circuit he'd ridden so often over the years—out to Dollar Butte and back again. Who knows what happened out there? There was some thunder far off and maybe a lightning flash spooked his horse.

Here George interrupts to say, Not that he couldn't stay on board a spooky horse. If there was a better hand with a horse in our part of the state, it was this woman sitting right here.

With the back of her hand Margaret shoos away the compliment. What do you do, Mr. Nevelsen, when you have bad news to deliver? George here used to bring the priest or a minister with him.

Jack Nevelsen nods his assent to this practice. I brought along the coroner a time or two. He's an old-time doc who knows everybody and they know him.

Margaret smiles tightly and continues, Back when

George was in office, folks had to know when the sheriff and a man of the cloth came up the walk, they better lock the doors and windows. Anyway. We got our news from a horse. James rode out on Honey, a barn-sour creature if there ever was one. Of course she'd come back to the herd first chance. George was the one who saw her coming and he was off the porch like a shot. We found James out by a twisty old juniper. He was lying there like he was left at the only landmark in all that empty prairie. With his neck broken. She sighs as though that tree has suddenly taken shape in her mind. He must have landed wrong. That's all I can think. Because he sure as hell got thrown plenty over the years and he climbed back on.

Jack Nevelsen nods solemnly. How much of life is that. Right there. Trying not to land wrong.

George, who has been listening to this story as if hearing it for the first time, says softly, Tell him about Janie. The phone call.

Margaret shakes her head but proceeds with the telling. James was a twin. Did George mention that? James and Janie. Though when this happened she was already living in Minneapolis and working behind a desk. With no intention to come back to North Dakota if she could help it. But that evening she called us, she who hardly ever called. But the phone rang and it was Janie. Was everything all right with James? she wanted to know. Buy yourself a train ticket, I told her. I'll pay you back when you get here. You've got a funeral to go to. Then I handed the phone to George. I couldn't bring myself to say any more.

Sheriff Nevelsen looks to George, who wanted this part of the story told.

George says, She had to know the fact of it.

And that was your job, Jack Nevelsen says.

George draws deep on his cigarette and nods. The smoke drifts from his nostrils.

No practicing for that work, Sheriff Nevelsen says, then steps back from the jail cell and looks up and down the corridor. He walks a few steps, retrieves a coffee can from under a bench, and uses it as a makeshift ashtray to crush out his cigarette. He holds the can out to George, who puts it to the same use.

The sheriff tugs at the brim of his hat as though he's about to step out into a stiff wind. I better get back to the house, he says. Nora can't talk to her folks any easier than I can, but together we can manage until they go off to bed.

Thank you again for your hospitality, Margaret says.

Hospitality. All three of them laugh at that word.

Well, says Margaret. I don't know what else you'd call it. Sorry I couldn't do better for you.

Margaret pats the mattress. Sheriff, I aim to sleep like a baby.

The sheriff points out the wall where the light switches for their cells are located. I'll leave the lamp on out in the office, he says.

Then Jack Nevelsen says good night and walks away from his guests in the Mercer County Jail. Neither George nor Margaret speaks until the echo of his footsteps fades and his key turns in the lock of the outer door.

Who's the man you thought you'd find in office here? asks Margaret.

Wesley Hayden.

Well, he'd have to have been something special to

outshine Mr. Nevelsen. Folks around here have got themselves a good one.

George nods in agreement. Though we might have loaded him up with more than he wanted to hear.

I was surprised you wanted him to hear about Janie.

To this George says nothing.

It sounded even stranger, Margaret says, when I said it out loud.

And what do you suppose your Sheriff Nevelsen would think, says George, if he knew you felt like you had to bring along a .45 and a box of ammunition on this expedition to find your grandson?

I have no idea, George. But if you feel the need, you can tell him tomorrow. Right now, I'm pooped. I'd like to make good on my promise to sleep the good sleep.

8.

AND SLEEP SHE DOES, BUT GEORGE, FOR ALL THE NAPS and nights he slept in Dalton's jail, lies awake. He chose the cell on the end, a room so narrow that when he lies on the iron cot he can reach out and touch the far wall and one of the large stone blocks that form the courthouse's foundation. Cold radiates from the stone. The light that Sheriff Nevelsen left on in the outer office can't find its way down the hall to where George lies. The smell of bleach and disinfectant stings his nostrils. Years of bodies have compressed the mattress into a shape that doesn't match his own. When he shifts, the rusty springs beneath him let out an anguished groan. If his door should slide shut, he'd be locked away from Margaret, sleeping in her cell two doors down.

After more than an hour of staring into darkness that doesn't vary whether his eyes are open or closed or whether he gazes into the future or the past, George gives up. He rises from his bed, dresses, grabs his cigarettes, and, stepping cautiously in case some forgotten obstacle might be in his way, gropes his way out of the cell and down the hall.

In addition to the disinfectant, there's another familiar smell here. Gun oil? Across from Sheriff Nevelsen's desk there's a rack with a 30-30 and two shotguns, handcuffs looped over the barrel of each. A new typewriter ribbon? Carbon paper? Ah, there it is. Right next to the door. A mimeograph machine with its distinctive pungent ink and paper, their odor the perfume of classrooms and public offices everywhere.

George steps outside, careful not to allow the outer door to lock behind him. He walks a distance away from the courthouse and the small, bug-speckled lighted sign declaring Mercer County Sheriff, as if it were trying to draw customers. The windows of the houses across the street are all dark now but one, and in that square of yellow light a shadow moves, someone for whom sleep is as hard to corner as it is for George Blackledge.

Autumn has come to northeast Montana. The vapor of one's breath, the clarity of the stars, the smell of woodsmoke, the stones underfoot that even a full day of sunlight won't warm—these all say there will be no more days that can be mistaken for summer. One might as well stand out here until frost whitens the ground and geese cry overhead.

George lights a cigarette and walks to the car. The condensation that will need to be scraped off by morning can at this hour be wiped away with a hand, which is what George does, right over the remnants of the block-letter *B* gas ration sticker, still not entirely scraped or peeled away, though six years have passed since anyone cared how much gas you used. He peers into the car's dark interior as though he expects someone might be on the other side of the glass, watching him. He takes out his key, unlocks, and opens the door, and, squatting down, does what he was certain to do all along, never mind the delays of stargazing, sniffing the air, or smoking a cigarette. He reaches under the seat and brings out the paper bag with the bottle of bourbon. Earlier today, he got no farther from the Roundup than his car when he broke the seal and a promise that had aged longer than the bourbon itself. But the whiskey had worked none of its magic then, and when George lifts the bottle to his lips now, it's with no more expectation than that the night's chill will retreat a little.

He caps the bottle and slides it back under the seat, right where it rode during his years in office. The .45 that was its companion, then as today, is no longer there. George transferred it to his suitcase when he and Margaret unpacked the car for their night in the Mercer County Jail.

A train's whistle travels easily on the night air. The tracks for the Empire Builder run through Bentrock, and the train itself stops at the station across from the Northern Pacific Hotel, not four blocks from the jail. George could leave the keys in the Hudson, and, before the sun rises and Margaret wakes, he could walk to the depot, buy his ticket, board the train, and be well on his way to Spokane, Seattle, Minot, or Minneapolis, depending on which way this train runs.

That's what he could do.

He flips his cigarette high in the air, letting its pinwheeling sparks imitate the stars. He walks back into the jail. Its dark corridors are no easier to negotiate than before, but he finds his way to Margaret's cell. A woman who sleeps without fear of locks, bars, or imprisonment, accidental or otherwise, she has left her door only slightly ajar.

George stands outside the cell, his hands gripping the

cold steel bars. His wife's slumbering breaths, slow-paced chuffs, bounce from one concrete wall to another.

Go back, George whispers. Go back. He aims this command squarely in the direction of her dreaming head. *Go back.*

9

THE BLACKLEDGES DON'T LEAVE BENTROCK AT FIRST light, as they told Sheriff Nevelsen they intended to do. Instead they eat a leisurely breakfast of sausage, eggs, and fried potatoes at the Bison Café, chosen because from a booth in the front window they can keep watch on Frontier Saddlery right across the street.

And when someone unlocks its front door and turns the sign from Closed to Open, George and Margaret rise from their unfinished cups of coffee and cross First Avenue in the middle of the block.

Inside the saddle shop a young man who looks as though he should be in algebra class slides a drawer into an old brass National cash register. He's unsmiling and slight, and steel-rimmed spectacles make his eyes, pale as twilight, appear even paler. His dark hair is combed tight to his skull, and his shirt is buttoned to his throat. He looks suspicious, unaccustomed as he is to early customers, especially those who have never walked through the door before.

But Margaret Blackledge's smile can calm most creatures, no matter how skittish.

Good morning, she says.

Morning.

George inhales deeply, as if the smell of leather is more welcome to him than Montana's open air.

When Margaret puts her wrist through the wood stirrup of an elaborately hand-tooled saddle and lifts stirrup and fender, the stiff leather creaks. That sounds like my knees when I got out of bed this morning. She lets the stirrup fall. You have beautiful saddles.

Yes, ma'am. Fellow in Miles City makes some of them. The fancy ones.

Very impressive. Wouldn't you say, George?

A hell of a craftsman.

Margaret squints at the inked numbers of a price tag. And not bashful either.

These are one of a kind, ma'am.

Oh yes. As I said. They're beautiful. Her smile widens. But we're not shopping for saddles.

The young man adjusts his glasses and looks over at a wall hung with tack.

Or bridles or bits.

And now it's apparent why all his buttons are buttoned. This is a young man too easily undone. He moves back and forth behind the counter like a horse not sure whether it wants to break from its stall or back up deeper inside it.

Would you be a Weboy too? Margaret asks.

No ma'am. But a cousin to. I'm a Tucker.

George asks, Donnie's your cousin, then?

Margaret's smile subsides somewhat when she looks her husband's way. But it shines brightly again when she turns in young Mr. Tucker's direction.

We're relations too, of a sort, Margaret says. Donnie married our daughter-in-law. *Former* daughter-in-law. My, family can get complicated, can't it? So Donnie's step-daddy to our grandson. We were up here in this corner of the state, and I said to my husband, Let's look in on Donnie and Lorna while we're here. Oh, I say Donnie and Lorna, but you know—doting grandparents. It was the boy we truly wanted to see. So imagine how we felt when we were told, Oh no, you don't want the Bentrock Weboys. Donnie's from down around Gladstone. But I was sure, just *sure*, that Donnie used to talk about his days in Bentrock. Margaret waves toward the ceiling of the shop as if it were twenty feet high and gilt-painted. He even talked about the store here. His uncle's? Do I have that right? Your dad?

None of what Margaret says is directed toward George, yet he walks away from her spell-casting anyway. He positions himself in the front window of the saddlery and surveys a gray, dusty main street not very different from Dalton's. The Cattleman's First National Bank, a squat brick building with two columns good for nothing but show. A five-and-dime. A Rexall's. The Bijou, where *Royal Wedding* will play at seven o'clock only. Two old men with their boots up on the bumper of a late-model Oldsmobile. And that car, like every truck or car passing or parked, wears a layer of dirt the color of coffee with cream, dirt that even a day of rain wouldn't wash away. Around Dalton the vehicles often wear orange-tinted dust coats, the residue from scoria, the volcanic rock present in the Badlands. Across the street at the Bison Café, the door opens, and when it does its glass releases a flash of sunlight like a knife blade. George returns to Margaret and young Mr. Tucker's conversation.

Yet I was sure, Margaret is saying, that Donnie said

they were relocating up around here because he could hire on as a hand on his uncle's place.

This here's his uncle's place, the boy says, taking in the store and all its leather with an owner's wave of the hand.

And we sure as hell don't see Donnie on the premises, do we, George?

No, we don't.

But didn't Donnie say his people had an outfit in Montana? And work was waiting for him?

The young man says, An outfit? More like nesters, I'd say. That'd be his folks' place down around Gladstone. Well, his ma's place. His dad passed away some years back.

Your uncle.

The young man nods. Not that Donnie's ma'll make him lift a finger if he ain't in the mood. And I don't know what kind of ranch work he'd be doing. They don't raise much of anything except old junker cars and trucks. And Cain, maybe. At this, young Mr. Tucker permits himself a smile.

Margaret winces. Oh, this isn't good. You're not painting a picture of a very promising husband or father.

The young man shrugs as if the truth must be borne no matter how unpalatable.

And of the two, Margaret says, it's how he'll do as a father that concerns us most.

Sort of the reason we want to look in on them, adds George.

Not that we don't care about Lorna. But you understand.

The boy nods as though the fitness of men and women for parenthood is a subject to which he's devoted considerable thought.

George, who once in motion lacks his wife's patience in

some matters, asks, The Weboy place down by Gladstone—
will we have any trouble finding it?

Hell, you let it be known you're looking for Weboys,
they'll find you.

Margaret, efficient gleaner that she is, understands
when there's nothing more to be found in this field. We'll
be on our way then. She wiggles her fingers in young
Mr. Tucker's direction. And thank you for this little chat.

The Blackledges are almost across the threshold of
Frontier Saddlery before the proprietor's son comes back
to his purpose. Chaps! he calls out. We got chaps too in the
back. And leather to special-make a pair if you like.

But they are on their way, leaving behind so many
empty saddles it looks as though every horse decided at
the same instant to throw its rider.

10.

FROM THE BLUFFS EAST OF THE CITY, GLADSTONE,
Montana, looks as though it could have been laid out by
a shotgun blast, the commercial and residential districts a
tight cluster in the center and then the buckshot dispers-
ing in the looser pattern of outlying houses and businesses
owned by those Montanans for whom space is a stronger article of faith than neighborliness. And farther from
the heart of town, trees are sparser until, beyond the city
limits, nothing grows higher than a tall man's knees, except for the cottonwoods near the glittering curves of the
Elk River. In the vast, arid distance are a few ranches, but
viewed from this height they could as easily be abandoned
as running.

On this plateau, near a tall knob of rock and clay
that looks like an upside-down bowling pin, George and
Margaret have parked and look down on their destination.

About the size of Dickinson? Margaret asks.

Hell no. Maybe a third as big.

Do you know anybody from here?

Del Wick.

Del at the hardware store?

George nods, a gesture lost to Margaret since she's

staring intently across the miles of riven sandstone and sage-brush. He's down there, she says. Jimmy.

You're sure of that, are you? They could be in California by now. Or anyplace between here and there.

Margaret shakes her head. That's what I thought before. But Donnie will stay close to his people. Especially knowing we're trailing him.

And how the hell would he know that?

You think the boy in the saddle shop wouldn't tell his folks we were in the store asking about Donnie? And they didn't phone down here and say we're on the way?

Maybe you're putting your feelings about family on others.

And what—you can imagine Donnie striking out on his own? Making his fortune for himself and his bride?

People change.

Do they.

I thought we needed to believe so.

Margaret walks to the edge of the bluff. Hardly a cliff's drop-off but still steep enough to snap an ankle with a mis-step. She kicks a stone and its clattering fall startles something into motion, a jackrabbit, probably, and it makes a scratchy echo through the brush.

There, by those cottonwoods, Margaret says, pointing down and to her right. That flatland. Where the creek or the backwater is. We could set up camp there.

If it's dry.

Well, you can see it is.

Is there even a road going down there?

Off to the right, says Margaret. Don't you see it? She points to a steep, rocky trail that widens, narrows, then widens again for no discernible reason.

Those rocks, George says. Good way to knock a hole in the oil pan. You sure you don't want to check in to a hotel for the night?

We have the tent. Might as well use it.

And save a buck in the bargain.

I can't believe you'd object to that.

George relents. I guess the ground can't be any harder than that jail cot.

He heads back toward the car, but when Margaret doesn't come with him he returns to the edge of the bluff. She's still looking westward at the town and the prairie beyond and he takes his place beside her. There they stand like the statues of pioneers who never face each other but always the new land.

After long moments of silence, Margaret steps close enough to press herself against his bony chest. Her tremor is a countermeasure to his heart's slow beat. We'll build a fire, she says. It'll be romantic.

Our last chance to be alone?

Something like that.

George puts his arm around her slender waist and pulls her tighter to him, but he's staring down at the area where she says they'll set up camp. His eye is searching for something to burn among all that sand and sage, where any log is likely to be petrified.

· · ·

Late in the day the wind rises, spinning around to blow hard and cold from the northwest. It snuffs out any thoughts of building a fire, and George has to weight each corner of the tent floor with the heaviest rocks he can carry.

George and Margaret eat their evening meal in the car,

out of the reach of a wind that would put sand and grit into every mouthful. Neither do they want the scent of their food to attract coyotes, cougars, bobcats, pocket mice, or wood rats. In the Hudson's silence they eat hard cheese, sausage, crackers, and carrots that have begun to go limp. They drink water from a canvas bag filled that morning in Bentrock, water that tastes neither of home nor of the place where they find themselves now.

At least another hour until dark, says George. We could drive in for a cup of coffee.

My, my. I've never known you to be in such a hurry to get to town. Usually you're in a hurry to get out.

Fifty yards ahead, two grouse whir into flight. With his index finger, George tracks their windblown, sideways course in the air. I should have brought a shotgun, he says.

Who quit first—me cleaning them or you killing them?

Not much point in one without the other.

To the end of my days I'll never forget that smell of dead birds. She wrinkles her nose. If the only meat I could eat was something I'd plucked the feathers from, I'd become a vegetarian.

Nobody cooked grouse better than you. There's a meal I'd eat every week if I could.

Oh, hell, I just smothered the birds in sour cream. I could have served you chicken and told you it was grouse and you wouldn't have been any the wiser.

I believe I could taste the difference.

Maybe you could, George. Maybe you could . . .

Margaret stares out the window, her gaze so vacant a bird could burst into flight right in front of the car and she might not even blink. Finally Margaret says, Much as I miss the ranch, George, there's something I don't miss.

Which is what?

Dead animals. Not so much the cows and the chickens, though I got so I had trouble lifting the fork to my mouth with a few creatures. Those I'd gotten to know maybe too well. But my God, George. We sure buried a few over the years.

George taps the steering wheel with his index finger as though he's counting to himself. That we did, he says.

When we had to put Strawberry down, I was afraid my heart couldn't take it.

You and that red roan had a lot of history.

I never told you this, but just before you put the gun barrel to her head, I put my arm around her and whispered in her ear. Remember? I said to her. Remember how you liked to gallop through the first snow every year . . . Remember when we raced Ernie Dahlberg and his big black mare and we left them choking on our dust . . . Remember when we were coming home on that September evening and the full moon was just coming up over Dollar Butte and you stopped like you cared about the moonrise as much as me . . . Remember when we put the twins on your back and you stood so still like you knew you had to take care of them . . . Silly, isn't it? That a woman who doesn't believe there's any world but this one wanted to send her horse on her way with happy memories . . .

She was the horse that took you to and from school?

She was. When she was just a filly. Bob Hildebrand and I were the only ones who came to school on horseback.

You think we didn't get some teasing about that? We were the country kids for sure. But not too many years before, there were so many of us who rode to school they had a little four-stall barn out back for our horses. Of course there were days Dad would ride in with us and then ride back at the end of the school day.

George listens to his wife talk about the distant past, but his eyes are fixed on distances of space. He gives a little nod, barely perceptible, toward a low hill to the northwest. Look out there. Must be eight, ten antelope. See them?

Margaret turns her head but she's still distracted by memory. Where?

He leans over and points with a gnarled index finger. See them?

Not really.

Well, they blend in pretty well. You recall seeing that young fellow we drove past on the way out of Ott's? He's got an uncle over in Medora who saw a mountain lion in his backyard last week. And he lives right *in* Medora. Said he stepped out his back door and there the cat was, eyeing him like he might be supper. When I look out at that hillside I think it wouldn't take much for a cougar to hide out there, since he's the same damn color as the grass.

But Margaret can't concentrate on the animals that might or might not be in the brush. She hasn't finished recalling the animals that crouch in her past.

And Patsy, says Margaret. Wasn't she something? She couldn't work cattle but she could sure as hell herd the twins. I'd see one of them wandering too close to the creek and I'd tell Patsy, Go get Janie, and quick as you please Patsy would take off. The next thing you know, she'd be turning

Janie around and steering her back to the house. She was a good dog, Patsy.

Too bad she couldn't herd someone else away from the creek.

At that remark, Margaret Blackledge turns in her husband's direction with such speed you'd think she was jerked on a string. Her eyes flash like the underside of a thundercloud, and she seems about to explode. Then in the next instant the string snaps, and she slumps as if she'd just heard grievous news.

Oh George. Her words come out as a moan. No. Not again. Can't you leave this be? After all this time?

He remains silent and looks out on the prairie in the same unfocused manner as his wife did a moment ago.

You never said a word to me back then. So why now? It was so long ago, George. Can't we put this away once and for all?

George rests his left arm on the steering wheel like a sailor willing to let the current carry his boat where it will. All right, he says, we'll stay put. I guess I can get along without my after-supper coffee for one night. But you tell me—why aren't you in a hurry to get into town? What if they're still on the move? You're not concerned that even one night could cool the trail?

Her arm stretches out along the back of the seat and her hand stops inches from her husband's hand. The sound of her fingers scratching at the upholstery is the same sound as the wind throwing handfuls of sand against the car.

I wanted to give you another chance, she says, to back out of this deal.

Now who's the one who doesn't know the other? I'd

follow you anywhere. If you don't know that, Margaret Mann, then what the hell do you know?

Did it ever occur to you that maybe I'd like you beside me and not behind me?

I'm the one driving this car. George moves the steering wheel a few inches to the right and left.

Margaret brushes cracker crumbs from the seat between them and slides over into the space she's cleared. She puts her hand on his thigh and those fingernails that earlier scraped at the Hudson's wool now play at the raised inside seam of his Levi's.

You *could* say you want him back.

George keeps staring out the windshield as if at a winding road he must steer their way along. Have you thought this through? Mumps, measles. Trips to the dentist. Report cards. You're ready to sign on for all that again?

Are you saying you don't miss him too?

A man can choose his words too carefully, and his hesitation can be worse than anything he might misspeak. Finally George says, Since you brought up Patsy's name . . . remember when she died? You mourned that hound harder than your own father. Yet you got past it. Yesterday you weren't interested in hearing my list, but here's another. Grief. It doesn't last either.

Doesn't it.

Not like when it's fresh. It turns into something closer to sorrow.

Margaret removes her hand from his leg and slides back to her place by the door. He's a Blackledge, George. He belongs with his own kind.

Listen to you. His own kind.

I'll tell you what, George. You want a trip to town so goddamn bad you can drive in right now. Drive in and drop me off and then you turn around and go back home. I'll do what I need to do and then take a bus back to Dalton.

What if they're not there? You'll chase them around the country on a bus? What if they go where Greyhound doesn't?

I'll walk.

By God, you would too. And when you finally learn that what you want to make happen isn't going to happen? What then?

I suppose that's exactly what I've never been able to learn, she says in her warbling voice. Isn't that what you've told me over and over, George? That I don't know when it's time to call it quits?

Their tent is staked to a square of earth no nearer than a thousand miles to an ocean, in any direction. Margaret has never seen a body of water wider than the Missouri, and so many years have passed since George crossed the Atlantic that the experience could as easily belong to dream as to life. Nevertheless, when wind rocks the Hudson, they both feel as though they are in a boat too small for the sea surrounding them on every side.

11.

THE TENT'S CANVAS POPS AND RIPPLES LIKE A FLAG ON A pole, the tent's interior is darker than last night's cell, and the ground is harder than the iron cot. Yet none of these prevent George from falling asleep. But at three o'clock in the morning, when the wind suddenly subsides and the tent's guy ropes cease to vibrate and hum, George comes awake as surely as if someone had shaken him. Margaret is sleeping soundly, her soft breaths steady and even and with not a sign of the tremor that troubles her waking hours.

George gives up even quicker than he did the previous night, and he carefully peels back the layers of wool covering him—half the blankets they own have been placed under them and half have been pulled over them. Grabbing his boots, George unties the tent flaps and slips outside.

He pulls on his boots and makes his way to the Hudson, the car's silhouette darker than the night. He eases open the driver's side door, takes the bottle from under the seat once again, and then, rather than slam the door, pushes it closed as quietly as he can. With nothing but whiskey to ward off the chill, George walks away from the camp.

On the western horizon there is a very pale smudge of light, little more than a softening of the dark, and the cause has to be the lights of Gladstone. So faint . . . yet enough to steer by. A man—or woman—could set out on foot and find the way to town.

He lights a cigarette, and he has taken only his second pull from the bottle when a voice speaks out from the darkness. You need it that bad, Margaret asks, that you have to get up in the middle of the night?

Want it more than need it. Couldn't sleep anyway.

Margaret comes forward to stand at George's side. She has a blanket wrapped around herself so she seems bodiless, just a face in the general darkness. Then she reaches out a pale arm. I'll have just a little swallow. Please.

George hands her the bottle, and Margaret brings it cautiously to her lips. *Ugh.* She hands the bourbon back to him. How many times have I said it? Mix a little burnt sugar with kerosene and I don't think it would taste a hell of a lot different.

George drinks again, then caps the bottle.

You don't have to sneak, you know. I never asked you to take the pledge.

I know.

So what's this all about, Mr. Blackledge?

I told you. I couldn't sleep.

Well, has it done the work you needed done? Are you ready to come back to bed? I need your heat in there, so even if you can't sleep, you can at least lie in there and radiate.

George drops his cigarette and grinds it into the dirt. He says, As long as I can be of some use. If any sarcasm or bitterness accompanies this remark it doesn't show in George's voice or Margaret's reaction.

Margaret turns then and leads them back toward the tent. It'd be a might easier to make this little trek, she says, if you hadn't brought up the subject of mountain lions earlier.

I'm right behind you.

Some comfort in that, I suppose.

As he follows his wife he looks back over his shoulder, the anxious glance of a man forever checking the night sky for any sign of daylight's approach.

12.

THEY RISE EARLY, FOLD THEIR BLANKETS, DRESS, AND drink a little water. They each eat an apple, and George smokes a cigarette. George takes down the tent, a much easier process than assembling it in the wind. They drive toward Gladstone under a sky so heavy and low it looks as though a gust of wind would release a shower of lead filings.

Any of these dirt roads, George says, could lead to the Weboy place. How the hell are we supposed to know? Do you have some sort of grandmother intuition that will guide you?

I'll ignore that wisecrack, Margaret says. We know it's a ranch, right? Why don't we ask at a feedstore? They might be able to give us directions.

And if Donnie's not spooked yet, that should do it.

Fine, George. I'm open to suggestions.

But her husband does nothing but drive until they come to the eastern edge of Gladstone. Nodding toward a Mobil station, he says, I'm going to fill up. And use the washroom to perform my ablutions.

You first, she says, then reaches over the seat for a hand towel.

The restroom smells of grease and brackish water, but its sink and toilet are reasonably clean, and the husband

and wife take turns washing up for the day. Without any agreement but that of the long-married, they each fol-low almost the same procedure in the gas station's single bathroom, though Margaret locks the door and George does not. They each stopper the rust-stained sink and fill it with water. They strip off their shirts and stand before the cracked, blackened mirror, George in his undershirt and Margaret in her brassiere. With the bar of soap resting on the back of the sink, the same soap that has cleaned the hands of truck drivers, vagrants, runaways, and other hard travelers, George and Margaret lather their hands, faces, necks, and armpits, then splash and rinse themselves with water cold from the faucet. Margaret's shiver is not so dif-ferent from her tremor, but before she puts her shirt back on, she combs out her hair.

When Margaret returns to the car, George asks, How long are you going to last without a real bath on this journey?

She's pinning her hair back up, and before she answers, she takes the last bobby pin from the row she's had pinched between her lips. I'm good for another day or two. As long as I don't lather up a sweat or roll around in the dirt.

George holds out a newly purchased map of Montana. He doesn't unfold it but points to an address and tele-phone number written in the border. The telephone book has a Weboy, he says. With a town address.

You've been investigating on your own . . .

And the attendant gave me directions. Can't miss it, he said. It's right under the new water tower.

Margaret cocks her head and reads aloud the tiny num-bers and letters printed in George's careful hand. Eight twenty-four Wilbur Avenue. Who said there wouldn't be a map to show us the way! She laughs. Thank you, George. She slides across the seat to kiss him on the cheek, its gray bristles as rough on her lips as a rasp. Just for that I'm going to buy you the biggest breakfast you can eat.

George drives away from the Mobil station and steers the Hudson down the four wide lanes of Humboldt Avenue, but just in case someone might be tempted to drive cows rather than cars down the street, the lanes soon narrow to two, funneling drivers into the heart of Gladstone commerce.

This town is like the Blackledges', only with brighter colored signs and two of everything Dalton has one of. Both a Chevy and a Ford dealer. A Sears and a Montgomery Ward. Burch's Fine Furniture and Sunvold's Home and Appliance Center. Red Owl and Lamont Wholesale Grocery. The Exchange State Bank and the First National. The Stockman's Hotel and the Prairie Rose Inn. Enough churches to answer any prayer and enough bars to satisfy any thirst.

Margaret points to a café next to Woolworth's. Let's give The Mint a try.

Because the cars and trucks are parked parallel to the curb rather than diagonally, George drives a block farther to find extra space to fit the Hudson into.

The breakfast crowd has thinned out at The Mint. Once again George and Margaret take a booth at the window, where they have a view of the street.

The waitress pours coffee, dark as molasses, into heavy crockery cups. This meal will have to do the work of two, so they order fried-egg sandwiches with thick slices of ham and fried potatoes.

After the meal, when George has lit his cigarette and they're both on a second cup of coffee, Margaret asks, Who did you say is from Gladstone? Del?

That's right.

And? Did he talk much about growing up here?

Said it was pretty rough-and-tumble. Farmers, ranchers. Railroaders. Now the oilmen, of course. All coming together here and not having much use for each other. But it looks to me like that's mostly changed now. And the businessmen have won the battle.

George signals the waitress for more coffee, and when she comes over with the pot, Margaret covers her cup with her palm. Any more and I'll get the jitters, whispers Margaret. Even worse than usual.

Once the waitress leaves, George continues. The way Del tells it, Gladstone used to have the biggest whorehouse between Minneapolis and Denver. Bigger than anything in Billings, though I'm sure that city had more than one. Anyway, the madam running the place was a real character. Rode around in a fancy horse and buggy. And if any of her customers wasn't paying his bill, she'd go park in front of his house and just sit there. And since everyone knew whose rig it was, you can bet she didn't have to wait too long for that debt to come off the books.

She sounds like a savvy businesswoman. Then Margaret reaches across the table and playfully nudges her husband's hand. But how about you, George? Didn't you and Harry Dwyer come right through here when you were trailing horses for Bob Paskow? Did you pay any visits to that woman's bawdy house? Did you, George?

Her husband's face flushes to the color of red brick. You know better than to ask me something like that.

Oh come on, George. A man has his needs. I know that.

So does a woman, he says and quickly turns toward the window as if he doesn't want to look at his wife's face in the wake of that remark.

Margaret reaches farther across the table, but George has pulled back. Isn't it time you took your own advice, George? Isn't it time you let some things go?

He slides out of the booth. I'll get the thermos, he says. See if we can get it filled.

Don't, George. Don't walk away . . . But he's already gone, leaving Margaret stretched across the table with nothing to grab hold of but her husband's empty cup.

13

THE ROUTE GEORGE AND MARGARET TAKE ISN'T THE most direct, but by a process of one- and two-block steps and by keeping the water tower always in sight— its great steel ball clearly visible even against the leaden sky—they find their way to Wilbur Avenue. Although the house wears no number, the dwelling that must be 824 is the oldest and smallest on the block. If the day were sunny, the house would be completely overshadowed by the water tower, and if the reservoir were ever to give way, 824 Wilbur Avenue would be washed away like a child's stack of sticks. The house is an unadorned box painted two shades of blue with a cement block for a front step and a lawn that's more dirt and weeds than grass, and that unmown for weeks.

George pulls to the curb near a man who is vigorously raking leaves and twigs out of the gutter and into the street. When George cuts the Hudson's engine, the man stops raking and approaches the car. He doesn't walk to either George or Margaret's side, however. He stands right in front of the car as if he's trying to line himself up with the winged woman on the Hudson's hood.

Margaret is the first one out of the car, and the man leans on his rake and asks, What can I do you for?

Mr. Weboy? Margaret asks.

Who's asking?

She smiles and steps forward with her hand extended. George, however, hangs back, buttoning his coat and turning up its collar, though the man in the street is in shirtsleeves. But then George's action has nothing to do with temperature.

Margaret Blackledge, she says, shaking the man's hand. She looks back to make sure George is keeping up. And my husband, George. If you're a Weboy, she adds, we're family. After a fashion.

How do you figure that? He shakes George's hand hastily, then turns his hungry attention back to Margaret. He must approve of what he sees because he smiles and relaxes his caution. Bill Weboy, he says. A cousin, are you?

Not cousins exactly. Our former daughter-in-law married Donnie. So he's stepdad to our grandson. That's pretty tangled up, isn't it?

Like family usually is.

The squinty, heavy-lidded eyes, the broken, misshapen nose, the cocked grin, the massive chin cleft off-center— Bill Weboy should not be a handsome man. But he is.

We thought we'd pay a visit, George says. Since we were in the neighborhood.

Since you're in the neighborhood, Bill Weboy says, his grin growing wider, and since you didn't find them up in Bentrock.

Maybe handsome has nothing to do with it. Maybe there's just something in the way a big man pushes out that barrel chest, rolls those wide shoulders, and works that jaw that looks powerful enough to bite through bone, maybe there's something in all that confidence and power that makes women curious and men jealous.

You heard we were coming, did you? asks Margaret.

A little birdie flew down here ahead of you. He pinches the air to make a beak. Cheep, cheep.

George asks, Will this trip be for nothing too? Or will we get to see the boy?

Is he always like this? Bill Weboy asks Margaret. In a hurry?

The older I get, says George, the more impatient I get.

My husband, Margaret says, likes to get down to business.

A hell of a lot of men are like that. Weboy moves his jaw as if words could be chewed. Can't wait to get to where they're going. Women, in my experience, would as soon take their time. Enjoy the ride, so to speak.

If the two of you are through discussing the male character . . .

Tell you what, Bill Weboy says, let's go inside and give the ranch a call. See if anybody's home. Hell, maybe you can drive out there this morning and see that precious grandson of yours.

He is that to us, Mr. Weboy. Precious.

Doesn't even need to be said, Mrs. Blackledge. No one doubts it for a moment. Bill Weboy starts for his house. Halfway there he stops and flings his rake onto what passes for a yard. He turns around to face the street once again. Lorna says she lived for a time with you two in a little town over in North Dakota. You run into problems like I got here? This was a dirt road up until two years ago, and it drained just fine. Then the city paved it, put in sidewalks, and those goddamn gutters and sewer grates. Which keep filling up with leaves and twigs. And ice. Then we've got to get out here and work to keep them clear or the goddamn street floods. And did we ever get to vote whether we wanted it paved or not? Hell no.

That's civilization for you, Margaret says brightly.

Didn't you used to be a public official? Weboy accuses George.

Used to be.

But you weren't in charge of paving the streets, were you?

I didn't much give a damn whether the streets were dirt or concrete. I was concerned with who walked or rode on them.

Bill Weboy's grin rivals Margaret's for its suddenness and its shine. Fair enough, he says. Follow me.

. . .

His home looks like a furniture store's idea of a home. All the pieces are in place. The comfortable stuffed chair and the maple rocker. The floor lamp and the coffee table. The davenport with the reproduction of an English country-side above it. The ceramic figure of the terrier. The woven rug, the needlepoint pillow. But not a sign of a pleasure or a habit, good or bad.

Had your coffee yet? Bill Weboy asks. I could put the pot on.

We're fine, Margaret replies. Thank you.

Well, make yourself at home. I'll call out to the ranch and see what their schedule is like.

Bill Weboy walks out to the kitchen and soon he can

be heard loudly asking the operator to connect him to a number.

Margaret whispers to George, No Mrs. Weboy?

George shrugs.

Can't be, she says and sits on the davenport. George joins her. For a moment Margaret's energy dips, and her eyes close longer than she'd like them to. When she opens them it's to a man sitting blankly beside her as if he were waiting for the doctor to come in and say whether or not the cancer could be cut out.

What? Margaret whispers. What is it?

George gives his head a shake so slight you'd have to be his wife to catch it.

What? She puts her hand on his wrist.

You don't want this man's help, he says softly.

I need someone's help. We can't do this on our own.

George Blackledge turns a slow, cool look on his wife but there are no words behind this expression.

Bill Weboy reenters the room, rolling the knuckles of one hand in the palm of the other. You two have plans for supper?

We surely don't.

How would you like to be guests of the Weboy clan out at the ranch?

We don't want to be any trouble, answers George.

No trouble at all. My sister-in-law wants to meet you. Says you can swap grandpa-and-grandma stories. And just between me and you, she's a hell of a cook. Wouldn't be surprised but that she's already got her hands in the flour, starting on a pie.

You'd have to give us directions. Margaret says this to

Bill Weboy but she looks expectantly at her husband as she speaks.

Weboy shakes his head. Not a chance. I could be the best damn direction-giver in the world and you still wouldn't find it. You'd be out there on Four Bridges Road and notice that not only do you not see four bridges, you don't see a single one. And Ditch Trail is so named because that's exactly where it ends—in a damn ditch. And you wouldn't want to take County K, even if it gets you there, because it'd take you twice as long. No, you make your way back here at four o'clock and you can follow me.

The sun finds a gap in the clouds and a way around the water tower, and light momentarily enters Bill Weboy's living room and shines on the faces of the aging man and woman on the couch. Light and shadow make them look as timeworn, riven, and hard as the bluffs hovering over this town. But in another moment the clouds shift again, the sharp light vanishes in favor of a general shadow, and a softness returns to Margaret Blackledge's features. Thank you, she says. We'll come back. We'll follow you.

14.

BACK IN THE HUDSON, GEORGE SAYS, I'VE GOT NO USE FOR that man.

I told you, George. We need him.

What the hell for? Now we know Donnie's people are here. We could ask around and see if we can get directions to the place.

Be sensible. We don't know our way around this part of the world. We could crisscross the prairie for days and not find them.

George says nothing but shakes his head slowly. He turns the key in the ignition and, though the engine catches immediately, he keeps turning and lets the gnashing and growling of steel and grinding gears make an argument for him.

Find me a drugstore, Margaret says. If we're going to be guests of the Weboys for supper, I need a few supplies.

Before he drives away, George Blackledge casts a long look back at Bill Weboy's house. The skies have shifted once again, and a flash of sunlight turns all the house's windows into mirrors. It's impossible to determine whether that's a man staring out from the kitchen or just a cloud shape reflected in the glass.

. . .

Margaret Blackledge paces back and forth in front of the cosmetic counter of Shaw's Rexall, Gladstone's Finest Pharmacy and Sundries, as if its display of creams, powders, lipsticks, and rouges is a puzzlement placed before her to test her knowledge of womanhood and self. A mirror on the counter invites customers to renew their commitment to illusion. This section of the store is redolent with perfume, floral, sweet, and pungent as the air can be only where it is closed in with walls and roof.

A clerk, an older woman as thin as an axe handle and with a similar curve to her spine, spots Margaret's quandary and hurries over to help.

Meanwhile, in the back part of the store, George wanders among the belts and trusses, the hot-water bottles and the enema bags, the shelves of Carter's Little Liver Pills, Kaopectate, Bromo-Seltzer, Phillips' Milk of Magnesia, of Cloverine and Rosebud salves. He seems not in the least mystified by this array but moves among the products as if he were there simply to total up the indignities that can be visited upon a human body.

After she has made her purchases, Margaret retrieves her husband and they walk back out onto the streets of Gladstone.

My goodness, she says. I guess it's been a while since I shopped for such things. I think I gave the clerk fits. What shade are you looking for? she asked me. Red, I just want red. But which red? she wanted to know. Margaret holds up her small bag as though it contained something foul. Maybe I should just gnaw my lips and pinch my cheeks and bring up a little color that way.

You don't need the help, George says. Never did.

Well, I guess I fooled you into thinking so.

On their way to the car they walk past a man who slows down and scrutinizes the Blackledges carefully as they pass. The man wears a rust-colored suede coat, polished hand-stitched boots, and a white Stetson. He has a moustache waxed and trimmed to arrows that point in opposite directions. Once they are twenty yards beyond him, Margaret wonders aloud, What was troubling Mr. Fancy Hat?

He spotted us for strangers, George replies. He'd like to know what our business is in Gladstone. I couldn't count how many times someone would call or come into the office to let me know there was a stranger in town.

But that was Dalton. In a city this size?

Stop me if I've told you this little tale before. I don't want to turn into one of those old men who can't go anywhere in his talk but where he's already been. After the armistice had been signed, our company had weeks in London waiting for room on a ship to take us home. I went out for a walk one day and I wasn't wearing my uniform. I never opened my mouth or did a damn thing that showed me for a Yank. At least I didn't think so. But damned if those English folk didn't take me for a stranger right away. I knew the look even then. And that was London. A million people probably. A town full of strangers, you might say. Yet when they saw me, they knew. I wasn't one of them.

Let's head back out to the campsite, Margaret suggests. Where we won't have anybody staring holes in us.

George and Margaret Blackledge continue down the sidewalk, making their way past stores and businesses whose windows mirror a sky that has less luster than glass. With sidelong glances the Blackledges check their own reflections, watching themselves as another might for any sign that says they do not belong here.

15.

WITH SO MUCH UNKNOWN IN THIS LIFE, HOW LITTLE IT
takes for a face, a grove of trees, an outcropping of stone to
become familiar. And how powerful is the lure of the familiar. Propelled by something close to instinct, George
and Margaret head back to their campsite to wait out the
hours until they are led to their grandson.

On the way out of Gladstone, George asks Margaret,
Maybe we should look into checking in to a hotel or motel?

Now? When we're looking at the possibility that we
might be heading home soon? With Jimmy?

The knuckles of both hands gripping the steering wheel
are chapped, cracked, and have bled a little, something that
happens to George every year when the cold weather comes.
They'll be like this until spring, spotted, flecked, and lined
with blood that dries black and looks like dots and dashes of
Morse code. He wears gloves when he works outside and he
uses Bag Balm—Margaret has said, Soften up those hands,
mister, if you want to put them on me—but no amount of
protection or emollient can keep his hands from drying out
like an animal's hide staked in the sun. George takes a hand
from the wheel as if to keep it from her sight.

Aren't you getting ahead of yourself? he asks. You haven't
seen the boy or talked to his mother.

Ahead of myself... what a strange sight that would be.

This is something you do, Margaret. Count a thing as done because you want it so.

And what do you think gets something done, George? Doubt? Worry? Hesitation? For God's sake, you don't get across the river standing on the bank wondering if you can do it. You get wet.

And not just your feet, I take it?

In response Margaret stares out the windshield, giving her husband nothing but her profile to contemplate. Into her sixth decade she still has only one chin, a matter of pride to her, no matter that it trembles. Her neck is long, though its tendons often look as taut as the ropes that held their tent stakes. Yes, a regal profile. Yes, a woman willing to plunge into any water, no matter how icy or swift, if she has a reason to get to the other side.

. . .

It's a rare Montana day. The wind that died last night has not resurrected, not yet, and George can follow the tire tracks that the Hudson pressed into the dirt earlier. He drives down the hill with caution, though the first trip has shown him that the car has sufficient clearance to make it without damage.

Here we are, George says, turning off the ignition. Home again. He pulls on the hand brake, though they're parked on level ground.

The car faces west, where the clouds have thinned enough to allow brief patches of pale blue to blink through. If this sky clears, George says, this will be a damn cold night.

He rubs his shoulder as if that's where the memory of last night's stony, sullen sleep resides.

Margaret ignores this. She's up on her knees and turned around to rummage through a box in the backseat. How about an apple? she asks. Or some of these carrots?

You're just trying to keep me regular, says George. The apples are mealy, and there wasn't much to those carrots when they were fresh. As far as I'm concerned you can throw them both out for the coyotes and the mule deer. But if there's any coffee left in the thermos . . .

You know there is, Margaret replies. It's right there on the seat next to you. Help yourself.

George picks up the thermos, shakes it gently to confirm that, yes, there's coffee, but he makes no effort to pour any. He says, I'm thinking what I should have done is find a phone booth and give Jack Nevelsen a call. See what he might know about Bill Weboy.

Margaret turns back around, munching on a carrot. What makes you think there's anything to know?

Just a feeling.

Well, he had you pegged. Public official indeed.

I'm sure Donnie's told him about us.

Poisoned the well, is more like it, says Margaret. And how would Sheriff Nevelsen have any information on Mr. Weboy?

George shrugs. A sheriff hears things.

And files them away.

Not something you can help doing.

So there they are. There they stay.

Memory cleans itself out sooner or later, says George.

Margaret rolls down her window and tosses out the

stub of carrot. Mr. Weboy has said he'll help us. That's good enough for me.

And I trust him about as far as I can throw him.

Of course we know you're a suspicious man.

George touches his finger to his hat brim. Guilty as charged, ma'am.

Margaret squirms in place like an impatient child. I can't sit here all day twiddling my thumbs. Let's go for a stroll. Breathe a little fresh air.

You're the boss, George says, opening his car door.

· · ·

With the rocky foothills and striated bluffs behind them, they walk west, across a sandy landscape whose only undulation is a long, subtle slope toward a silty creek. The tall cottonwoods near the water rustle even without the wind, and the lint from those trees snags in the sagebrush and gathers in the pebbly seams where, in another season, water runs.

George's long strides keep moving him ahead, and his wife has to scurry to keep up. Slow down, Stretch, says Margaret. I said a stroll, not a race.

He waits and she comes alongside him and hooks her arm in his. Did you lock the car? she asks.

You saw me do it not three minutes ago.

I thought so. But then I wasn't sure whether I remembered the act or the thought.

Yes, I'm all too familiar with that feeling.

I tell you, Mr. Blackledge, this growing old tosses up a new surprise every day.

To that he says nothing. It's an observation he's made himself too many times already. What's the use?

Gesturing vaguely toward Gladstone, Margaret says, My God. What would make anyone settle in such dismal, godforsaken country?

Exactly what some would say about Dalton. And more people live here.

But Dalton makes sense, she says. You stop short of the Badlands. But here? You just get across and then stop?

Assuming folks are moving east to west.

Well, certainly.

As I recall that was the argument your father made. About how Dalton was settled, that is.

He was right about a few things.

You won't get any argument from me.

Now, my mother, she didn't know how to pour piss out of a boot—

—with the instructions printed on the heel. So it's the day to quote Warren Mann, is it?

He never said it within her hearing, she says quickly.

You don't have to defend the man to me, Margaret. I thought the world of your father.

They walk silently for another hundred yards. The clouds have once again thickened and filled in the blue patches with gray and the hillside grass has lost its gold and turned tawny.

At dinner tonight, Margaret says, they might offer some sort of liquor.

They might.

If they do, I'd appreciate if you'd pass on the offer.

George Blackledge glances quickly down at his wife. The limitless, lowering sky, the long stretches of motionless empty prairie, the silence, complete right down to the absence of birdsong—who knows what decides a man to leave most of his words unspoken?

Margaret says, It's not that I think you can't hold your liquor. It's just that—damnit, I don't know. I'd like to create a certain impression, I guess.

Sort of like the preacher coming for supper?

Yes, she says. Exactly. I know you're poking fun at me but that's exactly what I want. After this evening's over I'll pour you a drink myself. Hell, I'll have one too.

Sounds like another bribe. Earlier you wanted to buy me breakfast and now it's a drink.

I'm not above bribing a public official, to use Mr. Weboy's term.

Former.

Former. Margaret turns her face to the sky. Is anything ever going to break loose from those clouds? It sure smells like rain. She pinches herself tighter to his side. Can I try one more time? Once more to see if I can make you understand why I'm doing this?

Make me understand?

She hammers his arm lightly with the side of her fist. Make you. Bribe you. If I could crawl inside your skull and fiddle with your thoughts . . .

You've already done that.

She strikes him again, this time with even less force. I'm afraid, she begins, two words that are as strange to George's ear as to her tongue. I'm afraid I'll just float away. She spirals her finger in the air. Like that cottonwood fluff. That everything the Manns have been, all the work my father did, and the Blackledges too, that it will all have come to nothing. Poof. Vanished. Gone. Nobody left on the land with the name that made the place what it was. What it *is*.

You're pinning a hell of a lot on a boy not long out of his diapers.

He's a *generation*, George. Don't tell me you don't understand that?

Nobody, says George emphatically, who ever met Margaret Mann—or Margaret Blackledge—could ever forget her. Or her name. Nobody.

She stares up at this somber man who is incapable of voicing something he does not believe. I'm not sure that's a compliment, Mr. Blackledge, but I'll take it as such.

Ahead, their flat path of sand and sagebrush runs up against the ascent of a hill, low but long, its crest lost to them.

Now let's head back, Margaret says. I want to dig out a dress and change before we return to Mr. Weboy's.

<u>16.</u>

On this windless day there's nothing to move them faster coming back than going out, nothing, that is, until they come within sight of the car and see a figure standing alongside the Hudson, looking in its windows.

Margaret is slower than her husband to break into a run, but she's the first to call out. Hey! You! Get away from there! And she soon catches up to her husband's stiff-legged lope.

The man at the car sees the couple running toward him, drops his fishing pole, raises his hands, and steps back from the Hudson.

Okay! Okay! All right! I'm not . . .

As George and Margaret come closer they see he's a young Indian man in bottle-green coveralls.

Halt! George issues the same command and with the same voice he has used all his life to make animals obey. Right *there*.

I didn't take nothing. I was just . . .

Even in his terror the young man wears a bashful smile. His dark caramel skin is smooth and untroubled. His thick, unruly hair is the blackest thing next to a crow's plumage in this landscape. He must be wearing warm layers under the greasy coveralls because the protruding wrists and ankles are stick thin, but his body looks bulky. His feet are shod in sneakers out of which water bubbles and oozes with each backward step he takes.

What? Margaret asks. You were just what?

Fishing? The young man stoops, picks up his fishing pole, and holds it out with two hands like an offering.

George walks over to the young man's tackle box and nudges it with the toe of his boot. Catch anything?

Hardly ever. He extends the rod farther. But I keep fishing. Every day.

Margaret tries the front passenger door of the Hudson. It's still locked.

I live over there, the young man says, pointing vaguely toward the northeast and the other side of the bluff. Got my own place. His smile widens but with worry. My own money too. I don't need none of your goods.

Margaret glances over at her husband, who is able, through some unseen force, to hold the young man in place.

Put down your goddamn pole, says George, and the young man obeys. And tell us why you were nosing around our car.

I didn't mean nothing. I seen your car here last night. So I'm wondering who's coming around here. Setting up camp and all.

You say you live near here?

Yes, ma'am. I walked down the same road you drove down. Without the pole in his hand, his fingers begin to rotate as they would if he were making a snowball.

What's your name? George asks.

Alton Dragswolf. Junior.

Margaret steps forward, and though Alton Dragswolf flinches, he stands his ground and shakes the hand she holds out to him.

George? Meet Mr. Alton Dragswolf. Junior.

Although he is still wary, George shakes the young man's hand too.

Margaret Blackledge, and this is my husband, George.

Alton Dragswolf nods as if he suspected as much.

Mr. Dragswolf, Margaret says sweetly, should we have sought your permission before setting up camp here?

Oh no, ma'am. This ain't my land. I guess I'm a little surprised none of the McWhirters came calling though. They can be real touchy about someone on their land.

And this is McWhirter land.

Yes, ma'am. They don't mind me because they know I ain't going to do nothing but take a few fish. But I don't advise camping here without their okay. And they won't give it. They won't let no one else's stock water here even. His smile is unceasing but Alton Dragswolf's eyelids droop as though he seldom gets enough sleep.

You certainly seem to know the area well, observes Margaret. Are you a lifelong resident, Mr. Dragswolf?

Lifelong? No, ma'am. Just all the life as I've lived so far.

Margaret smiles. So you might provide us with a little history—Gladstone history.

Alton Dragswolf keeps looking George's way, as if he worries Margaret's questions are intended to distract him from her husband's imminent attack. History? Yes, ma'am. I'm the one for history around here. I can tell you where the folks are buried who ain't buried in the cemeteries.

George speaks the name. Weboys?

Alton Dragswolf's grin doesn't diminish but he brings forth a scowl to accompany it. His face is dotted with moles so dark and evenly spaced they look as though they must form a constellation. There's a whole slew of Weboys, he says. And they been here as long as there's been a here.

You had any dealings with them?

The Indian shakes his head, and once it begins to move, its motion threatens to be as constant as that of his fingers. Only with another movement—Alton Dragswolf steps back again—can he stop his head. No, sir, he says. And that's just the way I like it. I go careful through life so I don't have any dealings with the Weboys.

And you'd advise us to do the same?

That's the other thing I'm careful of. Giving out advice. Alton Dragswolf takes a few more backward steps and says, I better get going.

Wait, Margaret says, picking up his fishing pole and tackle box. Don't forget these.

Thank you, ma'am. He takes them both and shakes his tackle box as if he needs to hear it rattle to be sure of its contents. You folks camping here tonight?

Not after what you told us about the McWhirters.

You're welcome at my place. If you turn right up there instead of coming down the hill you'll find me. It ain't much but it's mine. I can invite who I like or do whatever.

Margaret gives a little curtsy. Thank you, Mr. Dragswolf. You're very hospitable.

Sure, sure. And I didn't mean nothing with your car. Just wanted to make sure everything's okay.

One last thing, Mr. Dragswolf, Margaret says. Do you ever stop smiling?

He shakes his head again, this time an action that seems

as though it should be accompanied by a whinny. He continues to back up, and only when he's thirty yards away does he turn and jog off, picking a path between the rocks and scrub and up the bluff's cut slope.

Halfway up the hill, Alton Dragswolf stops and puts down his tackle box. While George and Margaret watch, the young man opens the box and extracts a long-barreled revolver. George starts to pull Margaret away but the way Alton Dragswolf raises the gun and waves it over his head shows he has no intention of firing it.

I had my protection! Alton Dragswolf calls out. I had my protection with me all the time!

In spite of the weapon in the young man's hand, Margaret waves to him. And then Alton Dragswolf laughs, picks up his tackle box, and continues to clamber up the hill.

Mr. Alton Dragswolf, Margaret says. Junior. A handsome young man.

George has his keys in his hand. Leave your car unlocked, he says, and see how you like your handsome boy then.

Oh hush, you old grouch. He seems like a well-meaning young man. Now open the trunk and let me dig out a dress.

I'm not changing my shirt for this affair.

I never thought it for a moment.

· · ·

While his wife changes her clothes in the front seat of the car, George paces a watchful circuit around the Hudson's perimeter. Obedient to his wife's command, he keeps his back turned yet he can't help but catch a glimpse of pale shoulder and a flash of paler thigh.

George walks farther away, then he takes out a cigarette,

tamps it on a thumbnail, lights it, and draws deep. He's neither the first man nor the last to learn that desire can't be quelled with a lungful of tobacco smoke. Distance isn't the answer either, and he returns to his earlier post.

The car door opens, then slams shut, and Margaret calls out in that tremolo that he knows better than his own steady breath. All right! You can open your eyes!

Margaret has traded her Western shirt and Levi's for a dark blue floral-print dress that she bought before the war. In place of boots she wears black high heels that bite into the hardpan. She bends down to look in the Hudson's side mirror and with the tip of her little finger she corrects a smudge of freshly applied lipstick, its red a shade that only newly spilled blood could match.

At the sound of George's approach, she turns and says, Can you believe it? I forgot to bring a slip! Then she lifts her dress until its hem rises to her knees and, laughing, swishes the fabric back and forth like a cancan dancer.

You're in good spirits.

I'm going to see my grandson tonight, George. That's what I came here for. And it wouldn't kill you to crack a smile for the occasion.

17

BILL WEBOY IS RAKING HIS GUTTER AGAIN, BUT WHEN George drives up to the curb, Weboy abandons the chore, heedlessly heaving the rake into his yard. He walks over to the Hudson and the window that Margaret is rolling down.

About time, Weboy says but smiles as he says it. One of you should ride with me and the other follow. I can tell you where we're going and why and that way maybe you can find your way back on your own. He takes his keys from his pocket and, turning his back on them, walks toward the sky-blue Ford parked in the driveway.

Go ahead, George says to his wife. He doesn't want me in the passenger seat.

Are you sure?

About what? Hell yes. Go.

Then she's out the door, trailing Bill Weboy across his scrubby yard and hurrying as much as those high heels will allow. Margaret's mackinaw lies on the car seat, and in fingering its wool George discovers that her purse is there too, a lump under the coat. Slip, coat, purse, a faint aroma of perfume—only the last what a sensible woman is apt to forget she has left behind.

. . .

They've not traveled any farther than a shift into third gear when Bill Weboy asks, So tell me, pretty bird—how long you been with that truculent old bastard?

Margaret turns in her seat and casts a quick, nervous look in the direction of the Hudson, barely a car length behind.

I don't guess I should answer, Margaret says, until I look up that word in the dictionary. But it can't mean anything good.

You'd know better than me, but he don't look like anything but hard bark.

Not that you seem truly interested in the answer to your question, Margaret says, but George and I have been together almost forty years. And Mr. Weboy? If you intend to use this occasion to do nothing but slight my husband, you can pull over right now.

Loyalty. Always an admirable quality.

Neither says anything again until they're out of Gladstone, heading west on a ruler-straight highway and rolling fast over land that beyond the barrow ditches is as flat as still water. Then Weboy asks, That old jalopy won't have trouble keeping up, will it?

You're looking often enough in the rearview mirror. You know where he is.

I guess he don't want you to get too far out of his sight. Which I understand. Weboy pulls a White Owl cigar out of his shirt pocket. Do you mind?

Your car. You don't need my permission.

He tears the cellophane with his teeth and teases the cigar out of its wrapper. Don't I? You strike me as the kind of woman a man is always asking permission of. Or excusing himself to.

An expert, are you? On kinds of women?

Weboy works his jaw around a thought. I've been around more than a few women who want men to ask before drawing breath.

Air's free and so are men. Work your theories elsewhere, Mr. Weboy.

Weboy clamps down hard on the cigar but leaves it unlit, though the Ford's interior reeks of stale cigar smoke and overheated motor oil.

I'll tell you a little tale about me and women, Weboy says. You saw my place, how tidy it is?

Yes. Very neat.

Well, that's all me. No woman keeps house for me. But not so many years ago it didn't look nothing like that. A regular pigsty. Or so my wife called it. She sniped away at me for years. Pick up after yourself. I'm sick of cleaning up after you. Oh, we'd go round and around. Just leave it, I'd say. Who gives a damn? I do, she'd say. Then her mother took sick, and Clara—that was my wife—was off to Idaho to take care of her. I'm leaving this house clean, Clara said, and I don't want to find it any different when I come back. Well, she found it different all right. I tore that place apart, every room, right down to lath. Opened it up good. Nothing left but rubble. And I did it all myself. Just me, a crowbar, a claw hammer, and Mr. Jack Daniel's. Clara came back, and the sight of the place scared the hell out of her. She saw to it I was locked up. For destroying something that belonged to me, if you can imagine. Then while I was behind bars, she cleared out. Left me with nothing but a bowl, a spoon, and a house without walls. Like men do, I thought if I changed my ways I could get her back. Got word to her that I quit drinking. That I was putting our house back together. You saw it—walls just where they're supposed to be? Plastered and painted?

Near as I could tell.

The hell of it is, once I was finished with the house, I was finished with her. Haven't had a drink since. And that house ain't ever anything but neat as a pin. The outside, I don't give a damn about. But inside—inside, it's just the way Clara would like it. Except she's never setting foot inside again.

So you destroyed your house out of spite and built it back up out of spite. You are either the most consistent man in the world, Mr. Weboy, or the least.

His laugh is a chest-deep rumble. He uses the unlit cigar in his mouth as a pointer, nodding toward a crossroad ahead. We're turning up there, he says. Heading for the hills.

A row of dun-colored low hills humps up to their left, but the flatland has already given way to eruptions of rock, as though the wind had scoured away the earth's outer flesh and exposed the bones beneath.

Instead of announcing it to me, Margaret says, why don't you signal so George knows what's coming?

Aye, aye, cap'n. Weboy clicks on the turn signal, and when the time comes takes the corner too fast, the Ford's tires squealing and the car wallowing on its springs. Margaret braces hard to keep from shifting closer to Bill Weboy.

The road—cracked, buckled, crumbling blacktop painted with neither center nor shoulder stripes—rises and dips through the hills, and Weboy pushes the Ford as hard going down as going up.

Outside of Weboy's line of sight, Margaret grips the armrest on the door so hard her fingernails bend against the metal. Tell me, Mr. Weboy, she says, when you're not keeping your house or your gutter clean, what do you do?

Oh, a little of this and a little of that. But nothing regular. I'm on disability. Brought malaria back with me from the war, and I can't be sure when it'll flare up again.

How about when you quit drinking? she asks. Did you do that alone or was it with Jesus's help?

That's a hell of a smart-alecky thing to say.

Just that I've heard more than a few ex-drunks in my time. And most of them want to give the credit to someone else.

Your husband one of them?

No, she answers quickly.

I did have some help. But it didn't come from Jesus. My sister-in-law hung in there with me when my own wife was ready to throw me to the dogs.

Good for her.

Damn right. Not many women—hell, not many men or women—have what it takes to grab a man by the collar and tell him right to his face he's got to straighten himself out.

Your sister-in-law . . .

Donnie's mother. Blanche.

Your brother—?

Weboy turns onto a gravel road, and his speed raises a cloud behind them. Even with the windows closed, Margaret tastes dust.

Dead since before the war, Weboy says.

I'm sorry to hear that. He couldn't have been that old.

Got himself a little bitty cut on his hand when he was

mending fence. Infection set in and he was dead just inside a month. Couldn't anybody hardly believe it. Since then it's Blanche holds the Weboy family together. Like I wouldn't be surprised same as you do with yours.

Not much work there. Only George and me in the house.

Only him to ride herd on? Hell, I'd quake too if I had that job.

Mr. Weboy. You've insulted my husband, me, and even our car, if I'm not mistaken. Why you are so determined to roil the waters is beyond me, but I've had about enough.

I've noticed you've got this talent . . . you can call a man mister and it sounds worse than if you'd called him a sonofabitch. He reaches his hand into the space between them, makes a tent of his fingers, and presses and kneads the cushioned seat as if it were cramped muscle.

You might not believe it, says Margaret, but I've been holding my tongue, or trying to. But by God you make it hard. Since you brought up my quaking, she says, I'll say a word or two about it. Doctors didn't know what caused it, but I have my own theory. I believe it might have started back when I used to keep my jaw clamped tight to stop myself from speaking my mind. The pressure would build up and when the words couldn't get out the quivering would start. So I resolved, just let them go. And that's generally what I do. If I've got something to say, I say it. But I've gone back on that with you, Mr. Weboy. I've been minding my manners with you. Now, we came all this way to see our grandson, nothing but, and while we appreciate the help you've offered, it doesn't give you reason to be rude.

Bill Weboy jerks his thumb over his shoulder. Looks

like your husband might be dropping back. I guess the dust got a little thick.

You could slow down.

Then it'd be longer until you see your grandson. Whom I've met, by the way. Fine-looking boy. And his mother is a good-looking woman. Donnie never asked me for a word of advice in his life, but if he had I might've told him to do exactly like he's done—marry yourself a widow, Donnie. You'll be getting yourself a grateful woman.

This is more of your wisdom of the female species, I gather.

Once you get to know me a little better you'll find I've got opinions on damn near everything.

I already know you well enough to know that.

Weboy runs his fingers slowly through his hair, the gesture of a man who's been told more than once what a handsome head of hair he has. You'll have to excuse me, Mrs. Blackledge. I can't help myself. People in this part of the world can be so damn tight-lipped I've just got to agitate a little to make sure I'm talking to someone with warm blood in their veins.

I assure you, mine is red and warm. You don't have to slice me open to look for yourself. Now, how much farther do we have to travel?

You mean how much more of me do you have to put up with? We've got three more turns to make, but we'll make them inside half a mile. See why I told you you'd need a guide? And here comes your husband now, staying right with us.

. . .

Stones clatter against the Hudson's undercarriage, and the car shudders over the road's washboard surfaces. Going into a bend, the wheels slide in soft dirt. But no matter how hard Bill Weboy pushes his Ford, George keeps pace, and through every hard climb, steep descent, and sudden curve he uses Margaret's silhouette to steer by.

18.

NO ONE WHO KNOWS BLANCHE WEBOY ONLY BY WAY OF words will be wholly prepared for the sight of the woman. She looks like nobody's idea of a ranch wife or a family matriarch. She is neither stout nor homely. She possesses neither gray hair nor broad shoulders. The woman who stands on the porch waving to the cars bumping across her yard is not much taller than a child, though she has a woman's cinched-in curves. Her long untamed hair is as black as Alton Dragswolf's, her pale cheeks are heavily rouged, and her wide slash of a mouth is brightly lined in scarlet. Her attire matches her complexion and her hair color—white blouse and black slacks. By the time George cuts the Hudson's engine, Blanche Weboy has stepped off the porch and is strolling out to greet her guests.

The house's two stories are an incongruity. With all this empty prairie on every side, why build up instead of out? But up it went, and maybe fifty years ago from the look of its weathered wood and approximation of Victorian design. The roof droops where a porch post is missing. An upstairs window is cracked. The screens are off the windows but the storm windows are leaning in stacks against the house. The mingled fetid and chemical odors of the outhouse and its quicklime travel too easily on the evening air.

Young Mr. Tucker was right: if anyone calls this place a ranch it's a term left over from a past life. Automotive horse-power looks to be the occupation now. Cars and trucks, their rusted hulls, bald tires, and grease-blackened parts, litter the grounds. These are more plentiful near the open door of the barn, as if they had either spilled out from that sagging, decaying building or were waiting to get in. From the low branch of a towering elm, the only tree on the prop-erty, an engine block hangs from a chain, and an old Ford truck sits underneath, its hood yawning open, apparently waiting for the engine to be lowered into it.

Blanche Weboy stops, puts her hands on her hips, and calls out, I hope you like pork chops!

As if she were speaking to an old friend, Margaret says, My mouth is watering already.

Bill Weboy makes the introductions, hands are shaken, and for a few moments the new acquaintances mill about and take turns looking up at the lowering sky and making comments about the weather—the human equivalent of dogs circling and sniffing about each other's hindquarters. From a nearby fence post a meadowlark makes its piping cry, and the pigeons in the barn coo an answer. Time to go in for supper.

They enter the house through the back door, and with-out apology Blanche Weboy leads them through a covered back porch so cluttered they have to step over and around shotguns, rifles, boxes of bullets and shells, snow shovels, coats, boots, bins of coal, cans of kerosene, haphazard piles of wood, stacks of newspapers and magazines, jars of nails, screws, nuts and bolts, and sagging cardboard boxes whose contents are kept from view. From behind a box or under a log comes a scurrying sound that could be a mouse frightened by all these footsteps.

In the large kitchen the guests seat themselves at a long wooden table on which the dishes and silverware have been stacked but not yet distributed to individual settings. Evening is coming on, and the only defense against its encroachment is a kerosene lamp on the kitchen wall. The kerosene burns with an oily odor, and its light wavers and struggles through a sooty chimney that has not been recently cleaned.

We got strung for electricity a couple years ago, Blanche says, turning up the lamp's wick, but I'll be damned if I'll pay their prices. Now, she says, who can I interest in a glass of elderberry wine?

They all refuse, though Bill Weboy finally lights the cigar that he's been chewing on.

Well, I don't mind drinking alone, Blanche says, and pours herself a generous glass. She pulls out a chair and sits down next to Bill. Then she lights a cigarette and without prompting proceeds with a history of herself and her family. Blanche Weboy was born Blanche Gannon, and her ancestors, originally from Illinois, filed homestead claims northeast of Gladstone before there was a Gladstone. The early days were hard. Blanche, one of eight children, lost an older sister to pneumonia, and a younger brother drowned in a neighbor's cistern. Another brother was thrown from a horse, broke his back, and was confined to a wheelchair for the rest of his days. An uncle froze to death when he was caught in a blizzard on the way back from town. Her father was bitten by a rattlesnake and almost died. Yes, a hard life, and not for everyone. Blanche's brothers and sisters lit out as soon as they could and never looked back. Only Blanche stayed, and now her children are the fourth generation of Gannons and Weboys born and living on Montana soil. When she says she hopes to count Jimmy Blackledge as a transplanted fifth, Margaret grows pale but holds her tongue. But who knows, Blanche continues, what Donnie and Lorna aim to do—you can't plan young people's lives for them, can you? But Blanche won't be surprised if they decide to stay in Montana. When she first met Henry Weboy—she was working at a dry-goods store in Gladstone at the time—he couldn't stop talking about heading for California, but Blanche figured she had more than a little to do with his decision to stay. And now Henry is buried in the same country cemetery as her folks and his.

While Blanche talks, Bill Weboy clarifies the relationship between himself and his sister-in-law. That might not be his intention, but the way he stretches out his arm along her chairback and rubs her shoulder first and then her neck and proceeds to graze his finger inside her collar and along her clavicle—all done so familiarly that Blanche neither leans into nor shrinks away from his touch—makes clear that she is to him more than just the woman who married his brother. Margaret Blackledge gives her undivided attention to Blanche Weboy, but George tightly interlocks his fingers on the tabletop and, throughout the chronicle of the Weboy clan, stares down into the dark structure his hands have created.

Blanche stubs out her cigarette and with one long swallow finishes her drink. Bill Weboy touches the corner of her lips as if he's blotting wine.

But you came here to eat, Blanche says, not to hear me yak. Bill, why don't you go call the boys in for supper.

Aye, aye, cap'n, he says, stands, and leaves to carry out her bidding.

To the Blackledges Blanche says, But I suppose you could tell a story not a hell of a lot different from mine. You got a ranch over in North Dakota, I understand?

Not anymore, Margaret says. We sold a few years back and moved into town.

Sure, sure. I knew that. Of course. Well, look around here. I've sold off all the livestock. We can do better selling car parts and scrap metal than running cattle or horses.

Back in the thirties, George says, we gathered up bones out on the prairie and sold them.

Anything to make a buck back then. Right?

Almost, replies George.

Blanche leans toward Margaret and whispers, How long have you had the palsy?

You can say it out loud, says Margaret. She puts her hand on George's arm. He knows about my condition. And it's not palsy. It's—oh hell, doctors don't know what it is.

Well, you know what, honey? You're too damn young to be trembling like that.

It seems to bother other people more than it does me. I can still thread a needle.

Bill Weboy returns to the kitchen. Trailing behind him are two somber, hulking young men in oil-spotted and grease-streaked clothing.

There they are, says Blanche Weboy. Meet the boys. The tall one's Elton and the other's Marvin. Marvin's older by ten months, which should tell you something about my ex-husband. Say hello to our guests.

They each say hello in curiously soft, high-pitched voices.

That's about the most you'll hear out of them all evening, Bill Weboy says. They're the strong, silent type.

Have we got any beer? Elton asks.

You know we do, his mother answers. But first you go wash up and change out of those clothes. I don't want our company to be sitting down to eat and smelling motor oil instead of my cooking.

The young men tramp out of the kitchen. Their distinguishing feature, aside from their bulk, is dark curly hair that grows low on their foreheads and close to their skulls like sheep's wool.

How's that Hudson running? Bill Weboy asks. I bet those boys would be willing to take a look under the hood for you. Tap a little here, tighten a screw there, they could probably get you a few more horses.

George Blackledge ignores this question and instead slowly stands and asks, Where's the boy? Where's Jimmy?

Blanche leans back and looks at him a long moment. Why, he's not *here*. He's with his daddy.

Margaret can't hold back. His father—!

George quiets her with nothing more than a hand raised a few inches from the tabletop. We came here to see our grandson. On George's cheeks white spots show as if, with anger, the skin had tightened and become thin enough for bone to show through.

Blanche laughs and looks to her brother-in-law. You mean they didn't come here to eat my pork chops?

As if following the newly-established convention that no one will be addressed directly, Bill Weboy speaks to Margaret. If you can calm that husband of yours, we can enjoy the evening. And you can still see your grandson.

When night comes on in a room lit by kerosene, any

flicker of the flame can give the sense that darkness is about to triumph. George sits back down and says, If you brought us out here for the sake of a joke . . .

Blanche Weboy's wide smile remains, but her eyes narrow warily. Your grandson's with my Donnie, she says matter-of-factly. He took Jimmy along to go pick up the boy's mother.

Now it is Margaret who looks to Bill Weboy for clarification. Lorna . . . ?

She's working at Monkey Ward, Bill says.

In Gladstone?

You didn't tell them? asks Blanche.

Bill shrugs. I thought maybe they'd be back by now.

We could've seen Lorna and Jimmy in *Gladstone*?

Blanche waggles her finger at Margaret. Now I'm feeling insulted. You really don't give a damn about my cooking, do you?

I just meant . . .

Maybe you're a Jew. Maybe you can't eat pork chops.

George interlaces his fingers once again. Neither he nor his wife say anything, and after a long silent moment in which the only movement is the shifting cloud of Bill Weboy's cigar smoke, Blanche laughs. Oh, breathe easy. Anyone who knows me knows I can't be insulted. Eat my pork chops or don't.

We'd certainly hoped, Margaret says, to meet Donnie's family someday.

Did you. Well, I thought we should meet too. Bill, as long as you're standing there you could pour me another glass of wine. Blanche points at George and Margaret. You sure?

I'm not much of a wine drinker, George says.

Something stronger, maybe?

He shakes his head.

How about you? Blanche asks Margaret. You a teetotaler?

Oh no, says Margaret. I take a drink of whiskey every year or two.

Bill Weboy sets a full jelly glass of elderberry wine in front of Blanche and then resumes his post leaning against the icebox.

Blanche says, A special-occasion drinker, eh? And this doesn't qualify? She raises her glass and sips delicately. The truth is, I thought we should meet and have a talk. Donnie thinks maybe the two of you don't approve of him. With her ability to smile and scowl at the same time, Blanche Weboy looks from Margaret to George and back to Margaret again.

George raises his head slowly and levels his gaze at Blanche. Donnie gives a damn what we think? I'm surprised to hear that.

Blanche slips a cigarette from the pack of Pall Malls on the table. By the time the cigarette arrives at her lips, Bill Weboy has stepped forward with a lit match.

I wonder, Blanche says, if you ain't been comparing Donnie to your son. And that's never fair to the living. They can't ever measure up to the dead.

Is Donnie working? Margaret asks.

He's not as mechanically inclined as Marv or Elton but Donnie puts in his time out in the barn. Blanche blows a stream of smoke Margaret's way. Not that Donnie needs to answer to you.

No, he certainly doesn't. And I don't have to talk up my son's virtues to you.

Blanche Weboy leans back in her chair and fans her face. Ho-ho! We better get some food in our bellies before this get-together turns into a real blood feud—the Weboys versus the Blackledges!

And we got numbers on 'em, says Bill with a chuckle.

As if his statement required illustration, at that moment the brothers Weboy clomp back into the kitchen.

Blanche arches her eyebrows. I better feed these boys or we won't be joking about a feud. Margaret, will you deal out those plates? Bill, you can pull those pork chops out of the oven. And they're probably dried out by now, so grab some ketchup and Worcestershire too.

The Weboy brothers seat themselves. Margaret and Bill do as they've been asked—she sets the table, and from the oven Bill brings a cake pan piled with pork chops. As soon as he sets it down, the brothers grab two chops apiece. Blanche walks around the table with a pot and puts a few boiled potatoes on every plate. The evening's vegetable—canned corn—is served from a large bowl. Blanche starts to sit down, then stops. She retrieves a loaf of store-bought bread from a drawer and puts it on the table next to the butter. We don't stand on ceremony around here, she says. Help yourselves and if you need something you don't see, just ask. If I got it, you can have it.

Blanche Weboy puts food on her plate but makes no move to eat. She watches her sons like a mother who restrains herself in case she has to give up her portions to her children. For their part, Elton and Marvin eat with such focused vehemence that any conversation would seem out of place.

A car's headlights sweep across the kitchen window.

The sound of a car's engine throbbing before a clunk and then silence. A car door slams and then another. George and Margaret look up expectantly, their knives and forks poised. In another moment, the back door rattles open and someone calls out, Anybody home?

It's Donnie . . .

19.

HE APPEARS IN THE DOORWAY, SMILING AND RAISING A finger to the bill of his baseball cap in greeting to the diners. His first steps forward clatter on the kitchen floor.

Goddamnit! his mother says. Don't come in here in those shoes! You're going to chew up this linoleum and it ain't even two months old!

The hell, Bill says. You still playing baseball?

We're playing until the snow flies, says Donnie. And come next spring we'll have a leg up on every other team in the league.

You'll need more than a leg up, Marvin says, if you don't want your ass kicked.

Donnie is not only the best looking of the Weboy brothers, his presence in the room puts a little polish on Marvin and Elton. Now it's possible to see how close those thick wooly curls are to a head of wavy hair, how near those sullen expressions are to pouting sensuality, to see how easily those low, heavy brows could translate to a brooding charm. It's even possible, looking from Donnie to his brothers to his uncle Bill, to imagine what the boys' father must have looked like. A handsome man.

Without untying the laces of his cleats, Donnie steps on the heels and kicks the shoes back out into the entryway, the dark cave that George and Margaret are watching so intently.

Hey! a woman's voice says. Watch it! Lorna steps into the kitchen's light. She's a slender, pretty woman who looks tired and mussed from a long day on her feet. Her hair has lost some of the wave that it no doubt had when she left the house this morning. Her lipstick has been chewed or licked away. Under her eyes are semicircles almost as dark as bruises. Both her blouse and skirt look a size too large for her. Lorna's holding her son, who clings to his mother as if she had fur.

Hello, Jimmy, Margaret says.

At the sound of her voice, the boy looks up quickly. Recognition flares in his eyes, but then, as if even four-year-olds understand that on some occasions they must stop themselves from speaking, he quickly puts his thumb in his mouth, hooking his index finger comfortably around his nose.

Uh-uh, Blanche says, and Lorna hastily pulls Jimmy's thumb from his mouth.

To Margaret, Blanche looks for affirmation. Am I right? Sure way to end up with buck teeth?

But Margaret displays no interest in orthodontics or child discipline. She has eyes only for her grandson. She rises from the table and walks toward the boy with her arms extended. Jimmy neither shrinks from her nor reaches out.

May I? Margaret asks Lorna.

Lorna shrugs her son from her shoulder and he goes willingly, letting his weight fall into his grandmother's waiting arms.

Jimmy. She kisses the top of the boy's head. I've missed

you so much, she says, closing her eyes and breathing in the child's essence. Jimmy . . .

A look passes between Blanche and Lorna, and though George seems to have caught it, Margaret is lost to any world outside the circle of her arms.

Relieved of her son's weight, Lorna stretches and massages the small of her back. God, she says, he's turning into a load. This she says of a pale, delicate, thin-limbed child who nestles into his grandmother's embrace without a wriggle or a complaint.

I told you, says Donnie. You pick him up too much. How's he supposed to learn?

Learn what? How to walk? He knows how to walk.

Hell, I'd probably unlearn how myself if someone would carry me everywhere I wanted to go. That's flat-out spoiling him.

Has he eaten? Blanche asks.

I bought him a hamburger at Ressler's. While we were waiting for Lorna.

And did he eat it?

About half.

Does he want a pork chop? Some potato? Blanche reaches over and tugs on Jimmy's foot. Do you? Can I cut up a little meat for you?

Without taking his head from his grandmother's shoulder the boy says no.

What's that? What are you supposed to say? Blanche yanks harder on Jimmy's foot.

The words are muffled because he speaks them into Margaret's neck, but Jimmy says, No, thank you.

To Lorna Blanche says, Take him up to bed then.

Lorna makes no attempt to take her son back from his grandmother nor Margaret to pass him back to his mother.

We believe, Blanche says to George as if he's the one who has an interest in the matter, in early-to-bed in this house. Blanche reaches up and pats Jimmy's bottom. And we believe in walking up the stairs on your own two feet.

Margaret backs up a few steps and tightens her hold on her grandson. Her eyes are open now, darting from one Weboy to another before settling coldly on Blanche.

Easy now, Grandma, says Bill Weboy, moving to stand between Margaret and the door. You know who makes the rules here.

At this remark George stands again, abruptly this time, his chair skidding across Blanche Weboy's new linoleum. Marvin pushes away from the table too but remains in his chair.

Then only the kerosene lamp's flame wavers. The room and its occupants are as still as a photograph, Weboys and Blackledges caught in a pose of wary readiness.

A gust of wind doesn't suddenly bang a door open. A clock doesn't chime. The phone doesn't ring. Yet in the next instant the stillness breaks as if it were made of crystal. Marvin drinks his milk. Elton spears himself another pork chop. Donnie's shoulders slump. Bill Weboy unwraps another cigar and lights it. What has passed in this room cannot be named but passed it has. Margaret bends down slowly and sets Jimmy back on his feet. When she does, he looks up at her with incomprehension, a child who, like most children, seldom understands why adults want to pick him up or put him down.

As if he's not been responsible for his own propulsion for a long time, Jimmy tests the floor under him, shifting from side to side and lifting one foot and then the other.

There was mustard, he says.

On your hamburger? asks Margaret.

He nods.

And you don't like mustard, do you?

He shakes his head.

The child has his grandmother's blue eyes but none of her smiling energy. He looks instead as if he, like his grandfather, would prefer to make shapes with his fingers and stare into their darkness.

Blanche claps her hands twice, and Jimmy flinches at the sound. Off you go, she says. Up the stairs.

It's been months, says Margaret, her voice strained, since we saw the boy.

More like weeks, Donnie says.

Well, says Blanche, now that you know how to find us, you'll have to visit more often.

Donnie shoves Lorna, and she lurches from the force, and then reaches a hand down to her son. Come on, Jimmy.

He slips his hand into hers. Anyone can see he is a child who will take any offered hand, lacking the certainty or courage to refuse it. As he and his mother walk away he glances back only once. A four-year-old has so little past, and he remembers almost none of it, neither the father he once had nor the house where he once lived. But he can feel absences—and feel them as sensation, like a texture that was once at his fingers every day but now is gone and no matter how he gropes or reaches his hand he cannot touch what's no longer there. His legs seem too thin for his body, and he can't gauge how to match his steps to his mother's.

Please, says Margaret.

When he hears the pleading tone in his wife's voice, George moves quickly. That's enough, he says, coming to her side and putting an arm across her shoulders. Enough.

Margaret keeps watching after her grandson, who has glanced back only once, his expression puzzled over this punishment he has done nothing to deserve.

Don't beg, George whispers to his wife, then steers her toward the door. To the assembled Weboys he says, We thank you but we'll be on our way.

Well, I guess we know who matters to you, Blanche says, standing and putting her hands on her hips. You're rushing off before the pie. But if you have to go, you have to go. Drive safe.

George and Margaret hurry as best they can through the cluttered porch and out the back door. Their eyes are unaccustomed to the darkness, total as only a cloudy night on the prairie can be. They stumble in the direction of their car, for the moment nothing but a black shape distinguished from the surrounding dark by its vague suggestion of substance.

Behind them a screen door slams and a voice calls after them. Whoa, wait up there, Blackledges!

Margaret keeps walking, but George stops and turns toward a white shirt hurrying their way.

It's Bill Weboy, who says, Just wanted to see if you needed to get pointed in the right direction. I'd lead you back to Gladstone but I'm spending the night here. Or maybe you're heading for home, back to your own side of the Badlands?

I can find the way, George says.

You sure? If you left a trail of bread crumbs, the coyotes have eaten them by now.

I can find the way.

If you say so. Bill Weboy looks past George to Margaret opening her car door. Running off like this, Weboy says, you hurt Blanche's feelings. She won't say so but I can tell.

Her feelings! *Her* feelings! Margaret leaves her door open to charge back toward Bill Weboy. The feeble light from the car follows her. We come all this way to see our grandson—*our* grandson, not hers!—and then she gives us two minutes before banishing Jimmy like a dog who pissed on her precious floor!

Bill Weboy raises his hands. Easy there, missus. Let's not forget our manners. I'm sure Blanche would be happy to play hostess to you again sometime. But she's trying real hard to get Donnie and Lorna squared away. Them two don't know much about raising a kid. Left up to them, he'd be up until all hours and eating ice cream for breakfast.

And are you out here now because she sent you to smooth my feathers?

Hah! If you think that, then you don't know Blanche Weboy. She don't give a damn whose feathers are ruffled.

Go back inside, Mr. Weboy, Margaret says. The night's cold and you don't want to catch a chill.

I sure as hell feel that. Bill Weboy pivots and walks away. Something in the night air, perhaps the vapor of breath, makes it seem as though that departing figure were puffing smoke, though Bill Weboy left his cigar in the house.

George, who has kept himself between his wife and Bill Weboy during their exchange, turns Margaret back toward the car.

They are inside the Hudson when Margaret says, His brother's wife indeed!

George turns the key to start the engine but Margaret

thrusts out a restraining hand. Wait! Look. In the upstairs window.

Silhouetted there is the unmoving shape of what is almost certainly a mother holding a child.

Margaret waves.

I doubt she can see you, says George. He shifts the car into gear.

Wait. For just a moment.

She's not locked up in the tower, you know. She married the man of her own free will.

But not his family.

No? A husband or a wife is usually a package deal. You know that.

Not you, George. You came unencumbered.

That I did. Then, without her permission, he drives away from the Weboy ranch.

Two miles will pass before the Blackledges will see anything rising higher from the prairie than the two stories of the Weboy house and its nearby elm tree, from which the auto engine hangs. Then the road will climb a rocky butte, its southern slope that hours before had been black with pines. When they descend they'll bisect the pastureland where cattle are bedded down invisibly among the grasses they grazed earlier. In another mile will come the turn they cannot miss if they want to find their way back to the main highway. Soon the steel skeletons of power lines will come into view. These and other landmarks George Blackledge had noted, as a man will when finding his way back is more important to him than traveling into new territory.

20

THEY DECIDE TO SPEND THE NIGHT IN GLADSTONE, AND after driving up and down Main Avenue and the surrounding business district they eventually return to the western outskirts of the city and the Prairie View Motor Court, accommodations that look as though they'll be cheaper than the Harrison House hotel or one of the three motels on the eastern edge of the city.

The night clerk, a bored-looking younger man who moves slowly and with the squeak of metal and leather because his shoes and lower legs are encased in braces, assigns them Cabin Number Eight, the farthest in a line of small, squat, whitewashed structures, though no other cars are parked in the lot. Cabin Eight, unlike Four, Five, and Six, has its own bathroom and its occupants don't have to use the outhouse, though they can if they like, the clerk adds with a barely concealed, self-satisfied smirk.

The cabin's interior has the same spare, tidy look as Bill Weboy's living room, and its mismatched furnishings might have come from estate sales. A bed with an old iron frame and a threadbare white coverlet. A low dresser made of dark wood and a painted nightstand. A rocking chair that might have once graced a front porch. A rag rug and a square of linoleum cover the warped wood floor, though not quite to the bare walls.

Tired as they are, the Blackledges unpack everything from the backseat of the car and bring into the cabin their pillows and blankets, boxes of groceries and other supplies. Since the experience with Alton Dragswolf, Margaret wants nothing visible in the car to tempt someone who might look in its windows.

As they unpack, Margaret talks about her grandson, explaining him to her husband as if George didn't have eyes to witness the boy for himself. What I noticed, Margaret says, was how much more grown-up he is. He understands more. I could see it in his eyes. I mean, he's always been a child who takes in everything, he's like his father that way, but now he's doing something with what he sees and hears. I can tell. He's *thinking*. And God only knows what he thinks about that house and its people. It can't be good for a child.

I didn't see any bruises.

Oh don't, George. You know what I mean. He's a sensitive little boy. Things affect him in a way they don't affect other children.

Those people in that house? One of them is his mother.

I'm aware of that, George. I'm well aware.

Finally, they retire for the night, the bedsprings squeaking out a reminder that though they are not yet home, they are no longer in the world of compromised sleep on jail cots or hard ground.

The evening's last words belong to Margaret. Do you need anything from Montgomery Ward? she asks. Because that's where we're going tomorrow.

· · ·

Lorna Weboy works in Montgomery Ward's men's department, the store manager's idea being that her pretty face and trim figure might induce a man who comes in to buy a suit to buy a shirt and tie as well, or a man who comes in to buy a handkerchief to buy a pair of pants to put the handkerchief in. That is where Lorna finds George Blackledge—looking at the handkerchiefs.

You'll find them cheaper in the catalog, she says, a remark that might have gotten her fired had that store manager heard it.

George reaches into the back pocket of his jeans and pulls out a snot-pasted, wrinkled blue bandanna. I'm pretty well fixed, he says.

By this time Margaret has come up on Lorna's flank. Hello, honey, she says to the woman who was once her daughter-in-law.

I didn't think you'd just go home, says Lorna. I almost said something to Donnie. If you believe you've seen the last of Margaret Blackledge, you'd best think again.

Like a bad penny?

To this Lorna says nothing. She takes a step back and crosses her arms.

Who watches Jimmy while you're working?

Who do you think? Donnie. His mom. Someone's always at the house. Or maybe you think I just tie him to a tree like a dog until I get home.

You're a good mother, Lorna. I know that. I was merely wondering how you're working things out with this job.

It's working out okay.

Did you drive in today? George asks.

Lorna straightens the stack of handkerchiefs that

George was examining. Uncle Bill gave me a ride. He and Donnie sort of take turns. Picking me up after work too.

Well, Margaret says, it sounds like you have a real system. Good for you. She pats the handkerchiefs that Lorna has rearranged. When do you have a break, Lorna? George and I would like to buy you lunch.

Lorna looks desperately around the store as if she's seeking the assistance of a coworker, someone who can help her with these customers who will never be talked into a sale against their will.

At noon, Lorna says.

Noon straight up? All right. We'll be out in front then. And we'll eat anyplace you like.

. . .

Nothing, not a siren nor a church bell nor a chiming clock hovering over the town square, marks the arrival of noon for the residents of Gladstone, but at the appointed hour Lorna exits the department store, and there, on the sidewalk under the brittle sunlight of late September and pressed against the bricks to stay out of the chill wind, she finds the waiting Blackledges. Together they walk across the street to Ressler's, where Jimmy was served his hamburger with mustard the night before.

Although the café is crowded with lunchtime diners, they're able to find a booth in the back, and once Lorna sits down, Margaret immediately slides in beside her, hemming her in. Lorna has put her purse on her left side, against the wall, and Margaret her purse on the right, so nothing is on the bench between the two women. On the printed menu the prices for pie, both plain and a la mode, have been inked out with a ballpoint pen and new prices written in. George points to these, shakes his head, and lights a cigarette. Soon a stout waitress arrives with her pad and pencil. She is scowling and grinding her teeth for a reason known only to her. George and Margaret both order egg salad sandwiches and coffee. Lorna asks for a hot roast beef sandwich and a 7UP.

Since I started working, Lorna explains, I'm hungry as a horse. Even though I don't do much but stand around all day.

You look as slim and pretty as ever, Margaret says to her. And good for you—working to help out the family.

I guess.

George offers her a cigarette, which she refuses. I only smoke the filtered kind now.

He leaves the pack of Lucky Strikes on the table within her reach.

Margaret extends a loving arm across Lorna's shoulders and tries to pull her close, an action that the younger woman resists. Margaret says, It's so *good* to see you.

You mean Jimmy.

I mean the both of you. Margaret pulls her arm away but her smile is unwavering. She says, But it took us a while to find you. We looked up north first. Didn't you say you were going to Bentrock?

I meant to write you.

I'm sure you did. But you didn't.

It was kind of a last-minute decision. Coming here, I mean.

Donnie's decision?

Lorna nods.

Well, we found you. That's the important thing. Jimmy's grown since we saw him.

He can count now. To ten. The wariness leaves Lorna's eyes as she talks about her son. At first he'd just say the words—you know, one, four, five, two—but now he knows they go in order. And I don't have to remind him about *please* and *thank you* any more. Even if he forgets, it's only for a second.

Margaret's delight at these announcements shows in her eyes too. He's so smart. Right from the start, so smart.

He misses you. Lorna's admission is shyly delivered. He talks about going to the park, like the two of you used to.

We miss him too. We miss both of you.

Donnie keeps saying we'll go back to Dalton for a visit sometime. But he never says when.

That's what I wanted to talk to you about, Lorna. And I won't beat around the bush. You're a smart girl. That was one of the first things James told us about you. You'll like her, Mom, he said. She's pretty and she's smart—

I thought you weren't going to beat around the bush. I have to be back at the store by one. Just get to it.

Margaret smiles in wry admiration for this young woman. All right. She places her palms on the tabletop as if to emphasize that she will keep her hands to herself. I'd like to propose something to you, Lorna. Here it is. Let Jimmy come back to Dalton with us. I don't mean for a visit. I mean for good.

Lorna's gasping, coughing little laugh helps her through her moment of speechlessness. Jimmy—! That's my son you're talking about!

You know we'd give him a good home. He'd—

You want me to give up my son? Is that what you're saying?

Margaret presses harder on the table. He'd have Teddy Christianson and Larry Ault as his friends again. Dr. Garber would be his doctor. Jimmy could walk to school—Dalton has good schools, you know that. He'd be in a town and a house that he surely remembers. He'd be back in his familiar world, back on our side of the Badlands—

Stop it! Just stop it!

When he's a little older, we'll take him to the cemetery. We'll tell him about his father and the name they share. I mean, I'm sure you'll do this too, but you're already a Weboy. And Donnie might be uncomfortable with—

The words come so fast Lorna presses her hands to her face. I can't *hear* this!

George and I aren't the richest folks around, but we can provide for him. Anything he needs—

All around the unceasing scrape and clink of cutlery and crockery, chewing, belching—customers have come here to eat and be on their way. There's still half a day's work to be done. The flare of a match. One last cigarette before hurrying back to the store or the office. Yet at this booth in the back nobody moves, not even when the waitress sets down the cups of coffee and the bottle of 7UP with the straw bobbing in it.

Eventually Lorna speaks. He needs his mother, she says. But the words come out as neither firm nor final; her voice betrays her and she asks the question that she doesn't intend. *He needs his mother?*

You know we'd give him a good home. You know that, Lorna. You know that in your heart.

In my heart . . .

Is it the mention of the human heart? The urgency in Margaret's voice? The expression of defeat in Lorna's eyes? Without contributing reason or feeling to the argument, without saying a word, George Blackledge picks up his cigarettes and slides out of the booth and walks away from the two women and their competing claims on a small boy.

Margaret gives her departing husband only a glance before focusing her gaze once again on Lorna. You and Donnie are starting a new life, she says. A new home in a new state. A new job. You're part of a new clan. And you and Donnie—I'm sure you want to start your own family. Blanche said—

At the mention of Blanche Weboy, Lorna's head suddenly lifts. What did she say? The smallest of waves appear on the liquid surfaces of the coffee, and the cups tremble in their saucers. The vibration comes from Lorna, who is bouncing her legs so fast under the table that everything above takes on motion as well.

Why, just that she wants the best for you, says Margaret. She wants to help you any way she can.

The hell. What she wants is Donnie where she can keep him under her thumb. I can fall off the face of the earth for all she cares.

Margaret puts her hand on the younger woman's arm, lightly at first and then tightens her grip, and this time Lorna makes no move to resist the touch. Come with us if you like, Margaret says softly. You and Jimmy. Live with us. Like before. We can take care of you too.

To the booth's inside wall Lorna turns her head as if she must look away from the older woman's gaze and its power to persuade and enchant.

Donnie'd kill me. Him and his mother . . . they wouldn't stand for it . . .

Margaret puts her hand on Lorna's chin and gently rotates her face back toward hers. Do you want us to talk to him? And to his mother? George and I could do that for you. We could take you back there to pick up Jimmy and your things and we can talk to Donnie and to Blanche. You don't have to worry about them.

Lorna tries to shake her head no, but Margaret's hand on her chin won't let her.

She won't let me go, says Lorna.

Oh, hell. You're a free woman in a free country. You can go where you please.

Lorna manages to move her head out of Margaret's grasp. She does so by leaning far back in the booth. I don't want him to grow up to be like Donnie's brothers.

They're a pair all right.

They don't even talk. Did you notice? I mean, hardly ever.

Margaret glances over at the space where her husband sat before he wrapped up his silence and walked away. I noticed, she replies.

Donnie's not like them. He's like his mom that way. The two of them—they're talkers.

So's the uncle.

Bill? Yeah. . . . He pretty much does what Blanche wants. Just so she'll feed him and let him under her sheets. I'm sorry but it's true.

You're not going to shock me, honey. Don't worry.

The teeth-grinding waitress returns with the two egg salad sandwiches on smaller plates balanced in one arm and the plate with hot roast beef in the other hand. She doesn't put George's sandwich down but asks, Is he coming back? Does he want this?

Margaret whispers, He went to the men's room.

Lady, he walked out the front door a while back.

Margaret looks toward the door, then gestures for the sandwich to be placed on the table. He'll be back.

Whatever you say. The waitress puts George's sandwich down and walks away.

Lorna pushes her plate away. I can't eat this.

Margaret nudges her sandwich toward the younger woman.

I mean I'm not hungry for anything. Lorna leans into her palm, holding her own chin the way Margaret held it only a moment ago. I need to think.

And now Margaret Blackledge shifts in position and attitude, opening up a space in the booth that feels vaster than the few inches between them. You need to think. That's fine. You think on this. Talk it over with Donnie if you need to or have a little heart-to-heart with just you and your soul. Are you working again tomorrow? Yes? All right. Tomorrow I'll come into the store, and all you have to do is shake your head. Yes if you've made up your mind, no if you need a little more time. Then if need be, I can come back the next day. But that's that. Then you need to say. Jimmy's coming back to Dalton with us, or you and Jimmy are. Do you hear me, honey? You'll have to say.

Lorna nods dumbly. I have to get back.

Margaret picks up the bill and slides out of the booth. We'll see you tomorrow then.

I guess, says Lorna.

For *sure*, answers Margaret.

21.

GEORGE BLACKLEDGE WALKS PAST WOODROW'S
Stationery with its line of typewriters and adding ma-
chines displayed in the window. Past Harmon's Western
Wear, Men's and Women's Clothing for All Occasions.
Past Antler's Bar and its odor of spilled whiskey and cigar
smoke that leaks out onto the sidewalk though the tavern's
windows and door are closed. Past the Remington Arms,
Rooms for Rent, Daily, Weekly, Monthly. At the end of the
block George stops and enters a telephone booth, on the
floor of which are at least ten cigarette butts smoked right
down to the desperate nub.

He takes out his wallet and a small folded piece of
paper. Written on it in a woman's handwriting are the
name Janie and two numbers, one for work and one for
home. He places the paper on the metal shelf, then weights
down each corner with the coins he takes from the pocket
of his dungarees.

He picks up the black telephone receiver but its weight
barely has time to register in his hand before he hangs it
back up. If it had been James's number on that slip of paper,
there might be some use in placing this call. James, with his
good-dog eagerness to please, would have been willing to
listen to his father's concerns. And James, who could make

his mother stop whatever she was doing and pay attention to him, might have been able to deter her from whatever course she was embarked on. But Janie? She was George's brand of Blackledge, someone who usually looked for—and found—a way to slip loose of any human entanglement.

Besides, every parent knows that it's his duty to listen to his child's fears, desires, and discontentments and not to burden his child with his own. He might forget this, so great is his need to unburden himself to someone who might listen, and understand, for the time that he has coins in his pocket. But soon he remembers. A parent remembers.

. . .

Margaret Blackledge finds her husband half a block away from the restaurant, smoking a cigarette and watching a man on a ladder paint something on a second-floor window above the State Farm insurance office.

What was the matter in there? Margaret asks. Your stomach or your nerve give out on you?

George's jaw knots but he says nothing.

I brought your lunch. She holds out the sandwich wrapped in yellow-stained napkins. If you want it.

George takes the sandwich but it's obvious from the way he holds it he has no intention of eating it. What'd she say?

She'll think about it. Imagine. Giving up your child. Walking out on your husband. And she'll *think* about it.

Don't be too hard on her. You can be very persuasive.

Margaret Blackledge looks up at her husband as though she can't be sure of his sincerity. Her scrutiny lasts a long moment but finally she gives up. Well, it didn't take much.

Just a minute. Leaving her husband?

She touches George's arm lightly. All right. I should have said something to you. I told her she could come back and live with us. Her and Jimmy. Like before. I don't think she'll do it, but last night when I saw her standing at Donnie's side, she didn't look none too happy. And how could she be—with that big baby for a husband? Living in that house with those wooly-headed louts lurking. And that harpy presiding over the castle. I had to say something.

Did you.

I'm sorry. I should have talked it over with you.

George points to the window he's been watching. A tooth, he says. They're painting a tooth on the window. A dentist's office. Sure. He looks down at his wife. I guess maybe we'll need a bigger house.

I said I'm sorry. I don't think she'll do it. I really don't.

He waves off her distress. We'll manage.

. . .

They spend the afternoon in and out of their car, wandering around Gladstone, and since the town is not their home everything they see and hear they compare to home. As they drive down Main Avenue they notice that the saloons have more business than any in Dalton would have on a weekday. In Dalton those three young women would never stand outside the drugstore openly smoking cigarettes. George and Margaret go into the Red Owl just to check prices and find not only that bread, milk, eggs, coffee, and hamburger are sold for less but also that the shelves are stocked with brands and products unknown in their grocery. And in the dairy section, margarine is available as well as butter. Because George didn't have lunch they go to Wolf's Bakery to buy him a doughnut and see rhubarb among the racks of pies, whereas in Dalton the bakery sells only the pies—lemon meringue, blueberry, peach—that women are unlikely to bake themselves. No one would presume to sell a rhubarb pie, unless at a church bake sale. They park the car behind the high school and watch the football team get ready for this week's game against Miles City. They have enough players to run a full scrimmage— eleven on a side. At Dalton High School they're still play- ing eight-man, just as they did when James and Janie were students there (and James was on the squad). The asphalt shingles used for siding on houses. The porch columns on the houses on Russell Avenue. The blacktopped elemen- tary school playground. The height of the steeple at First Lutheran Church. The size and ostentation of the newer houses along the eastern bench. The *Gladstone Gazette* published six days a week instead of the Dalton paper's two. The rows of trailer homes waiting on the town's western edge. The paving stones in front of the courthouse, the height of the curbs . . .

Finally the Blackledges have enough evidence to reach a conclusion: life could not go better here than in their town. They're certain of it.

22.

Late in the afternoon Margaret suggests they return to Ressler's for supper.

Was the food that good? asks George.

I can see Montgomery Ward from there, and I'd like to find out who picks Lorna up this evening.

What does it matter?

It doesn't, all right? But I'd like to know.

Ressler's is much less busy for the evening meal than it was at noontime, and George and Margaret are free to sit where they like. Once again they find themselves behind a plate glass window staring out at a street both strange and familiar. George turns the menu over in his hand as though he's searching for something not printed there.

Nothing look good to you? asks Margaret.

I've eaten more restaurant food in the past couple days than I have in the last five years.

Oh, you miss my cooking—is that it?

It sits a little better with me.

High praise indeed from Mr. Blackledge. She reaches across and taps his menu. Go ahead. Order a steak.

You're still buying, are you?

Call it a celebration.

She only said she'd think about it.

I'm optimistic.

Well, you were there. I wasn't.

The same waitress who served them lunch approaches with her pad and pencil. What'll it be? she asks. As she waits for their order the only sound is the grinding of her teeth.

Margaret asks, Does the split pea soup have ham in it?

Sizable chunks. And enough that you don't have to go looking for 'em.

That's what I'll have. And coffee.

George asks for the hot roast beef sandwich, just what Lorna ordered earlier in the day.

You gonna stay and eat it this time? the waitress asks.

And coffee, he replies. Black.

I'll bring it. It's up to you how you drink it.

As she walks away Margaret shakes her head. She'll have me grinding my own teeth before long.

Must be a hell of a life, waiting on folks.

I don't give a damn how hard your life is. It's no excuse for rudeness.

Maybe that plays here.

Maybe it does.

They fall then into the companionable silence of the long-married, content to wait for something new to enter their lives and the conversation to continue. Their coffee arrives, but still they stare out the window. Finally Margaret says, You're better at this than I am. God, I hate to sit around and wait.

George wraps his fingers around his coffee cup. You remember Bill Henning?

The father or the son?

It's the son I have in mind. Billy, I should have said.

I remember them both. And I went to school with Billy's mother, Dora Henning. Dora Armsen she was then.

And do you remember that I arrested the son? He'd been breaking into people's garages and sheds and stealing tools. He had a fellow up in Williston who was willing to buy anything and everything Billy could bring in. Anyway. When I think of waiting, I think of him. Once I found it was him doing the break-ins, I drove out to his folks' place and parked in a stand of cottonwoods and just waited. A stakeout I guess they call it now, but then I was just waiting. I did that for a couple hours every day. A week went by, and Billy never showed. But I kept on waiting. Because I knew sooner or later I'd see him going in or coming out. After a while I damn near hoped he wouldn't come back. Don't do it, Billy, I thought. Don't come back home. I don't know why. I had no special liking for the kid. It was sort of like feeling sorry for the mouse you've set a trap for, I suppose. And sure enough. He came back. And when I had the cuffs on him and was transporting him to the jail, I asked him, Where you been? Turned out he'd been up in Canada. Out in Washington State. Traipsing all over the Northwest, spending the money he'd saved—saved, mind you—from selling all those stolen hammers and saws and wrenches. And why'd you come back? Damned if he could give an answer. Never gave it much thought. He'd ended up there all his life. This was just one more time. The wrong time, I thought. But I don't believe I said that to him.

Such is the pull of home, says Margaret.

Is that what it is? I thought maybe it was the pull of needing to be punished for your crimes.

It might seem as though their silence has returned,

because Margaret says nothing for a long moment. She looks at her husband and leans her trembling chin into her palm. You're a patient man, George. That's one of your strong points. It was what made you a good father.

Did it. And as a husband?

Patience is always a virtue.

Well, right now I'm getting damn tired of waiting for that roast beef.

Did the Henning boy do prison time for taking the tools?

Three years in Deer Lodge.

There's a lesson in patience.

Is it patience when you've got no choice in the matter? I suppose.

Their order arrives, and George hunches over his food and eats like a man who's had only a doughnut since breakfast. But Margaret's attention is so focused on the double glass doors of Montgomery Ward that she can barely look at her soup long enough to bring a spoonful to her lips. George is scraping the final smear of gravy from the rim of his plate when Margaret says, There she is.

Lorna has just walked out of the store and stands on the sidewalk. She glances quickly in each direction, then leans back against the building. She reaches into her purse and takes out a pack of cigarettes. With the practiced efficiency of one who has lived in the wind all her life, she pivots, ducks her head, and, inside the sheltering cup of her hands, lights a cigarette.

For a few minutes she stands there, waiting tiredly, unaware that she's being watched.

Long day of being on her feet, says George.

Are you feeling sorry for her?

I am not.

She's not having an easy time of it. I know that.

Before Lorna's cigarette is smoked down to its filter, her ride arrives. Bill Weboy pulls to the curb.

Lorna sees him and his blue Ford. There can be no doubt of that. But for a moment she doesn't step forward. She remains in place as though some impossible comfort in the rough red bricks prevents her from pushing away from the building. But finally she moves, flicking her cigarette toward the gutter as she climbs into the car.

See that? Margaret says. She's in no hurry to—

To what? Go back to her child? To her husband?

Or mother-in-law. Or that spooky old house.

She's tired, Margaret. Or maybe she's disappointed that Donnie didn't show up to take her home. Donnie and Jimmy.

Margaret pushes her bowl away though a few spoonfuls of soup remain. We'll have to repack the car, George. We're going to have an extra passenger or two on the way back home. I'm sure of it. Extra passengers and their luggage.

23.

AFTER SPENDING SO MUCH OF THE DAY IN AIMLESS activity, the Blackledges relish having tasks to perform. They rearrange the tent and its poles, and they undo the neat piles and packets of towels and bedding and stuff them into corners of the Hudson's trunk. George takes the dishes out of a box and puts them in his suitcase, layered between articles of clothing. Through this process of re-packaging and disposing, they come up with a few empty boxes and cartons, and these they tear apart and put into the incinerator barrel behind the motel along with the food that can spoil or go stale. Margaret steps back from the Hudson and though most of their possessions are still in their cabin, she surveys the car as though it were fully packed.

If we have to, she says, we can put a suitcase or two on the front seat between us and Jimmy could ride there.

Hell, you can hold him on your lap all the way. It's not that long a trip.

At this suggestion she smiles. Of course she could do that. Of course.

Should we check out in the morning? George asks. Or wait until Lorna makes up her mind?

The clouds that have raced across the sky all day have

turned invisible with the approach of night. A few stars wink high above the eastern horizon. Now that she's stopped working, Margaret has to wrap her arms around herself against the evening's dropping temperature. We'll check out, she says.

. . .

George is sitting in their room's only chair. He's reading the day-old copy of the *Billings Gazette* he picked up in the motel office. Waiting on his tongue is the news about a man who died in a grain elevator in a small Montana town near Bozeman. Tongarden was the man's name. Hadn't there been a rancher south of Dalton named Tongarden? The dead man was forty-seven years old. Wouldn't their Tongarden have been about that age?

But when Margaret comes out of the bathroom George's question and his curiosity about Tongarden vanish. She's wearing a white nightgown with a scoop neckline trimmed in floral lace interwoven with satin ribbon. It has a center placket with shell buttons, and Margaret has left the top two buttons undone. The bottom of the nightgown has pintuck pleats, and the hem is finished with ruffles. She bought the nightgown at DeLancey's in Dickinson, North Dakota, one autumn over twenty years ago, after a particularly hot, dry summer on the ranch. She'd never spent that much on nightwear, and perhaps never that much on a single item of clothing, but at the time drastic action was in order. The money was well spent. The nightgown has never failed to have its intended effect.

George says, You brought that.

Hell, I brought damn near everything I own.

But *that* . . .

Oh, quit gawking, and let's have that drink of whiskey.

It's late September but when Margaret wears the night-gown you can see that her throat and a V extending down her chest are still red from the summer's sun.

You want me to water yours down? asks George.

Don't bother. Once I get the first swallow down, it'll be fine.

. . .

Margaret Mann rose from the floor, naked, unashamed as only a long-legged, slim-hipped, high-breasted nineteen-year-old can be, sure of her body and its utility, worn to little more than muscle and bone from doing a man's work on her father's ranch. George started to get up too, but she pushed him back down. She walked first to the back door and then to the front, locking each in turn. The message was clear. Neither of her parents carried a key, so Margaret and her suitor would carry this act to its conclusion even if her parents returned early from their Sunday afternoon dinner at Mount Olivet Lutheran Church in Dalton and stood banging on the door, howling to be let in.

Only this could stop them: Margaret lay on her back, her thighs gripping George's midsection, but before she allowed him to enter her, she grabbed his hair and lifted his head from where he was lapping at her breasts. She clasped her hands tightly to his face, looked directly into his eyes, and said, You're not my first. Breathlessly he re-plied, As long as I'm the last. And who, after all, is the man who can turn back when he's come that close to ecstasy? His answer was good enough for both of them.

When it came to the penchants and practices of women, George Blackledge was not completely without experience; he'd been in the Great War, and in the company of two other soldiers he'd paid for a woman in England and later had one all to himself in Belgium for nothing but gratitude. But those encounters did nothing to prepare him for Margaret Mann. He had no idea a woman could or would ride as hard in pursuit of her pleasure as Margaret did. In the midst of the act she reached overhead and with both hands gripped the carved wooden foot of her mother's heavy horsehair couch, moving it an inch or two in her passion.

Neither was George ready for what happened when they were alone together the very next day. They were in the barn, where Margaret's father or Sam Easley, the Manns' other hired hand, might walk in at any moment, and within earshot of Mrs. Mann in the house.

Look here, Margaret said to George. She walked over to a patch of sunlight flooding down from the hayloft. Then she unsnapped her shirt, dropped it to her waist, and turned around to reveal her bare back to him. On each shoulder blade she had a red spot about the size of a silver dollar, matching friction burns from lying with him on her mother's rug. Saddle sores! she said and laughed. I got one on my butt too but I won't show you that one. Not now anyway!

. . .

Forty years later Margaret Blackledge née Mann still has the passion and strength to set furniture moving. She reaches overhead and with both hands grabs on to one of the bed's iron spindles. As George drives himself into her she lifts and arches her body to meet his thrusts. The bed frame bounces and bangs against the wall and the springs squeal like a small trapped animal. The chenille bedspread has slipped to the floor.

Finished, his weight off her, the draft that has found its way into the cabin cooling her sweat, Margaret says, My, my, Mr. Blackledge. I guess this Montana air agrees with you. All eight of the nightgown's buttons are undone and its ruffled hem is bunched about Margaret's waist.

If we have Jimmy and his mother living under our roof, we won't have much in the way of privacy.

Margaret pulls the nightgown over her breasts and swings her legs off the bed. I wouldn't worry about that. We've always found a way to tuck ourselves away from prying eyes, haven't we? Maybe we'll sneak out into the yard under the dark of the moon.

I'm not much for that sort of outdoor foolishness. I guess I never was.

Margaret sighs. I was making a joke, George. A little levity, that's all. You certainly lost your mood, didn't you.

She heads for the bathroom and George lies back, staring at the ceiling so hard it can't be the ceiling he's looking at. But whatever he sees there, he must eventually tire of scrutinizing it, because when Margaret returns he's asleep. His arms and legs are splayed out in an attitude a little alarming in a man George's age.

. . .

Is it the wind, which can never be calm for long in this part of the world and has now found something unlatched or untethered to set free and send banging its way across Montana? Or is it an hours-later echo of the bedpost that George and Margaret had thumping against the wall?

Knocking. Steady and insistent.

By the time they win their struggle against the under-tow of the unconscious and sort out their dreaming impressions from more-likely sources of the sound, a voice accompanies the knocking. Mr. Blackledge? Mrs.? We have an emergency here!

The door, someone's at the door. In the middle of the night.

George sits up, clicks on the lamp at the bedside, and then flinches at the sudden light. He stands and although he's dressed only in pajama bottoms he walks quickly to the door and opens it without question.

24.

Yes, there can be no doubt—George opened the door. He opened it, and isn't an open door—whether open three inches or three feet—as good as a spoken invitation to enter?

But if George's assumption was that someone from the motel office would appear in the doorway, he was wrong, and before he can push the door closed—an effort that would have been futile anyway, considering what his pushing strength would have been matched against—four Weboys have shouldered and shoved their way into Cabin Number Eight of the Prairie View Motor Court.

First through the door are Marvin and Elton, the wooly-headed Weboy brothers, followed by their uncle Bill.

What the hell, George says. What the *hell*. He backs up a few paces, which is a mistake, since the Weboys immediately flow into the space he has vacated.

Blanche Weboy then enters, and slowly, as if she wants to be certain the way has been prepared for her. She looks around the cabin as casually as if she's inspecting it for her own use. Then she closes the door and slips the locking chain into its track, something the Blackledges never bothered with.

Margaret is sitting up in bed now and about to get out,

but when Bill Weboy looks at her and arches his eyebrows, she sits back, pulling the sheet up to cover herself. It has taken her an uncharacteristically long time to speak, but she finally says, You can't come in here!

Too late for that, Grandma, says Bill. We're in.

Blanche smiles and points to George. He opened the door to us.

What time is it? asks Margaret, but plainly she doesn't care what the answer might be.

So many bodies, large, light-absorbing bodies, in this small cabin, and their wavering shadows make it seem as though the room were lit by firelight.

Out, says George. Get the hell out.

Blanche ignores him and instead sits down on the edge of the bed. She doesn't even look at Margaret. See, you think you can gang up on Lorna, Blanche says, but then when it's done to you, it's a different story.

One of the Weboys—Elton? Is he the taller one?—moves to the door but only to stand with his back to it. The other brother remains in place. He's holding a canvas satchel that bulges as though it might hold a load of tools.

Blanche unties her scarf, takes it off her head, and waves it in the air. Then she sighs and shakes loose her black hair as if it has pained her to have it covered and controlled.

What are you talking about? asks Margaret.

Is that what you're going to do? says Blanche. Pretend like you don't know what I'm talking about? Pretend like you didn't jump Lorna at work? Two against one—

Nigger fun, her son adds.

—and the two of you badgering and bullying her to give up her boy. Shame on you. Trying to pry a baby loose from his mama. Blanche switches her scolding gaze to George. Shame on the both of you. You're lucky Lorna doesn't have a little mama bear in her. Come between that kind of mama and her baby, you're liable to get your hand bit. And worse.

That's not exactly what happened, says Margaret.

Somebody would have tried to come between me and any of my boys? Would have tried to talk me out of my own child? I tell you, it would have been hell to pay.

That's not—

So maybe you want to try again. Blanche twists her body around on the bed as if she intends to lie down next to Margaret. Maybe you want to present your argument now, when the odds are a little closer to even.

Fear can visit anyone, but on some people it can never stay. By now Margaret Blackledge has summoned back the nerve that is as much a part of her being as the color of her eyes. Is Lorna here? Margaret asks. Have you got her outside in the car? Because I'm only discussing this subject in her presence.

No, no, no. Blanche waggles her finger. You'll discuss it with me. And you'll stay away from that young lady.

Those are not decisions for you to make.

Aren't they? Blanche swings a leg onto the bed. If Margaret were up and dressed it might be noted that both women wear Western boots, though Blanche's are lustrous black leather, decorated with white stitching and stamped with floral designs.

Bill Weboy walks about the room, inspecting it casually

as if he needs to confirm an impression. His movement sets his nephews in motion, and they also start circling the room. Gradually Bill makes his way to the side of the bed and stands so close that his legs touch the mattress.

Flanked and hemmed in by Weboys, Margaret jerks the chenille bedspread and says to Blanche, Get your goddamn feet off my bed!

Blanche does not obey. Instead she moves around on the bed until her back, like Margaret's, is against the iron spindles of the frame. I think, Blanche says, we got off to a bad start, you and me. We should have talked about raising our own kids before we jumped off into being grandparents. Now me, I've always believed in letting my children find their own way once they're grown. Of course, I only had boys and that might have colored things. What did you have—a girl and a boy? So maybe you thought different how it should be done. Maybe you think you always know what's best. I understand that. But wouldn't you agree—even when you see them making a mistake you have to butt out?

Bill Weboy leaves the bedside to wander around the cabin again. He peers into the bathroom and into the open closet. He walks to the dresser where George's suitcase lies open and though he doesn't disturb the contents he examines them closely, looking up at George from time to time as though he hadn't truly understood the man until he inspected George's socks, his underwear, and his carefully folded but frayed and faded shirts and dungarees. For George's part, he keeps his own gaze fixed on Bill Weboy.

Margaret edges away from Blanche Weboy. I didn't say it was a mistake for Lorna to marry your son.

Oh-ho! I never said you said!

Bill returns to the bedside. Lorna picked your boy, he says and nods toward Margaret. Then yours, he says to Blanche. You'd think you two could meet on that common ground.

Margaret's tremor has worsened in the last minute, and when she speaks now her words totter as though she hasn't found where to put the weight that will balance them. I'm tempted to say I don't give a damn what Donnie and Lorna do. As far as I'm concerned they're free to find their way or get themselves lost. It's Jimmy I'm concerned with. He had a good home when he lived under my roof.

And now he's under mine.

How strange the enmity between these two women! It couldn't be any plainer in this cabin if it whirled visibly in the air like dust, yet at this moment they glare at each other across a distance that could be closed with a kiss.

Their stalemate and the silence it engenders—the arguments can barely be cogently thought, much less mouthed—provide Bill Weboy with an opportunity. By God, now I recognize this place. I used to bring a lady here. She was from Miles City, but when she was sneaking around behind her husband's back she didn't want his back anywhere near. Even coming here she wouldn't park her car out front.

When was this? asks Blanche.

Take it easy. This was a few years back.

Maybe we don't need to hear about your life as a Casanova just now.

Bill shrugs. Can't say I blamed her though. Her husband was a sonofabitch of the first water. I understood her coming here. I just didn't understand her going back. He reaches down and slips his index finger inside the neck-line of Margaret's nightgown, right between her shoulder and her collarbone. You know what I'm talking about, don't you, Grandma?

If, in his attempt to attack Bill Weboy, George had taken the shortest route—across the bed instead of around it—he might have gotten his hands around the man's throat, as he perhaps intended. But that path would have had him clambering over both Blanche and Margaret. As it is, going around the bed costs George an extra second or two, and he never makes it to his target.

Margaret is so quick scrambling down the bed that she seems to be reaching toward George at almost the same instant his blood begins to flow.

But of course she's too late to do anything but pity him.

And of course George was too late—too late, too old, and too slow—to get at the man who had his hand on his wife, before Marvin Weboy—or was it Elton?—struck him hard on the side of the head with a rubber mallet drawn without notice from that canvas bag. So now George sits on the floor at the foot of the bed—where he went down hard on his knees, then pitched forward and hit his head on the frame, opening a gash above his left eye—stunned like a cow before slaughter, bleeding, and not quite able to comprehend the many choices, steps, and missteps that brought him to this position.

Bill Weboy hasn't moved from the bedside. He takes a moment to contemplate George's predicament, then smiles and walks to the bathroom. He comes out with a towel and hands it to George. You don't want to get blood on the floor. That'll cost you extra for sure.

Margaret reaches through the iron spindles and touches George gently on the top of his head. Recognition comes into his eyes like a sunrise. Margaret. Blood. The floor. The mallet that clubbed him and the wooly-headed young man who wielded it. The older Weboy who stands above him as if George were merely something else that needed to be cleaned out of the gutter. George rises unsteadily.

Blanche Weboy is lying on the sheets that he and Margaret tangled in their lovemaking. You want to try again talking this over like reasonable folk, she says, or would you prefer to get some sleep so you can get an early start back home tomorrow morning?

Bill Weboy has returned to his post beside the bed, and he stands so close you'd think he was Margaret's protector rather than her tormentor. He reaches down and gives the bed covering a tug, something that Margaret is sure to feel. Or maybe, Bill says in a voice pitched low for Margaret's ears, you'd like to send him home while you stay on for a spell. I could take you back when you're ready. Of course, by then you might decide you'd rather stay.

In her own lowered voice, Blanche says to her brother-in-law, Let's keep to the matter at hand.

Meanwhile, George has staggered back and is leaning against the dresser, and the Weboy with the mallet moves over next to him.

Margaret twists herself around on the bed as if she's unsure of where she should direct her attention. Should it be toward Blanche, whose languid pose is calculated to conceal her claws and fangs? Or toward Bill, who never stops smiling, even as he's poking at her with a thick finger? Or George, who's still bleeding and appears woozy? But she and Blanche are the ones in the boat, and it's to Blanche that Margaret finally turns. I want, Margaret says, to take Jimmy back with me.

Blanche laughs. I know what you want! Christ, woman!

Not for a visit. For good. I want Jimmy with me.

Is this how she gets her way? Blanche says to George. She just stays with a thing until everyone else gets tired and walks away? Blanche sits up, bringing herself so close to Margaret that she must feel as well as hear the heat of Blanche's words. Well, I don't give up. And I don't walk away.

And you think I will?

Blanche sighs and shakes her head. Then she looks to Bill and points tiredly to Margaret as if signaling that he can now take a turn at persuading her.

But George has not been as dazed as everyone seems to have thought, and he has not been standing by the dresser only to steady himself. He has groped around inside his suitcase until his hand found the gun's hard shape.

Would he have used it only to threaten? Or would he have fired it immediately? And if so, at whom? Bill? Blanche? Probably not the Weboy standing closest to him—Marvin, definitely Marvin—and that is a mistake, for it is Marvin, still holding the heavy rubber mallet, who first sees the gun, Marvin who strikes George a second time, and even harder than before.

Once again George falls, and the blow causes him to loosen his grip on the pistol. It slips from his hand and skids across the linoleum and under the bed.

Get it! Get the gun! Blanche cries, though she is the quickest to it, jumping from the bed and reaching under to bring the .45 out from that dark space. Goddamnit! she says. Hold on to him—and see to it he can't pull the trigger!

Blanche's commands are so swift and so swiftly understood and obeyed that it seems as though all the participants must have planned and even rehearsed what happens next in Cabin Number Eight.

The Weboy brothers grab George's hand and wrist and roughly lift his arm in the air. George's legs are awkwardly folded under him, so he can do nothing to push himself away from the brothers' grasp. Besides, the brothers don't seem interested in hauling George to his feet but only in raising his arm. He tries pulling back but he's no match for the strength of the two young men.

Margaret has barely moved toward George before Bill Weboy grabs her hair, her long gray hair that she unpinned before she came out of the bathroom and climbed into bed with her husband. He pulls hard and Margaret topples backward on the bed. Then he hurries to help his nephews.

One of the Weboy brothers lets go of George's wrist long enough to push the suitcase off the dresser. Then the brothers jam George's hand—or at least three fingers of his hand, since one brother has a hold of George's thumb and little finger—against the dresser's edge.

Shit—watch out for my fingers, says a Weboy.

Then it is clear. As if the shadows had been pushed back to the corners, everything is clear.

Look out then, says Bill Weboy as he raises the hatchet he's taken from the canvas satchel.

And before Margaret can call out, before George can summon the burst of strength that might enable him to pull back, pull back before it's too late, the blade falls, passing through the skin, blood vessels, nerves, muscles, ligaments, tendons, and bones of George Blackledge's index, middle, and ring fingers, severing all three just above the base knuckles, before burying itself in the dresser's soft pine.

George's grunted *Ooohh!* sounds born not of pain but of exertion, as if he had torn his own fingers from his hand. And the groan must sound familiar to Margaret, who heard something similar rush out of him earlier in the evening.

25.

THE WEBOYS RELEASE GEORGE AND HE SLIDES DOWN again, watching, as he goes, his three fingers, which seem to hold on to the dresser for an instant before they lose their grip—or so it seems—and slip to the floor. Bill Weboy kicks at them but strikes only one and it skitters against the wall.

To Blanche, Bill Weboy says, All right. He won't be pulling a trigger again. Weboy drops the hatchet back into the canvas satchel.

Instinctively George clasps his left hand over what's left of his right and raises both of them to slow the blood flow. He presses both hands against his chest. The blood leaking out from his hands catches in the white hairs of his chest and creates a webbed pattern.

He looks up at Bill Weboy and through gritted teeth says, You cocksucker.

Bill Weboy smiles and puts his finger to his lips. Language like that? Not in front of the womenfolk.

My God, my God, Margaret says. By now she has arrived at her husband's side, and she takes his hands in hers and presses them to her abdomen. Blood seeps into the white cotton muslin and the stain spreads so quickly it seems as though the blood were flowing out of her. She falls to her knees in front of him and when George sees the blood on her nightgown he pulls his hands away and falls back against the dresser. Oh my God. George . . .

Blanche is standing over them now and the .45 is in her hand. She dangles it by its trigger guard as if it were an object whose purposes were a mystery to her.

I'll tell you what's going to happen next, Blanche says, and her words seem as practiced as everything else that has happened in the past few minutes. You're going to get him to the hospital quick as you can. And while you're there and the doctor is working on Mr. Blackledge, we'll be at the sheriff's office. Stanley Munson is his name. We'll rouse Stanley from his bed, and I'll tell Stanley what happened here. How your husband pulled a gun on us, and how rough things got, and how we took it away from him, and what happened in the process. For proof, I'll put the gun on Stanley's desk. Now, Stanley and I go way back. He's a good man and he'll listen to what I have to say. By the time he talks to you, he'll know the whole story. How you came here looking to take a child away from his mother. First with sweet talk and then with a gun.

Blanche bends down close to the Blackledges. Of course it'll be up to Stanley and the state's attorney but I'll try to convince them to let the two of you go on back to North Dakota.

She stands up again. Because I don't think you're going to make any more trouble here, are you?

Without being given a command to do so, the Weboy brothers and their uncle start backing up toward the door. Blanche pivots smartly and follows them. In the open doorway she stops and looks back at the Blackledges. Lorna told me you don't even go to church. And yet you think you're the ones who ought to be raising that boy.

Then the Weboys are gone, and for a moment Margaret holds her husband close, pulling his head to her breasts. Oh George, she wails. What have I brought us to! What have I done! What have I done to you!

You haven't done a goddamn thing to me. Not yet, anyway. But you're about to. You'll have to drive me to the hospital.

Margaret throws her mackinaw over her bloodstained nightgown and pulls her boots on over her bare feet. Together they manage to get George's dungarees on, and Margaret covers his bare shoulders with his shirt. Then they both discover something about what the coming years will mean, though neither says a word about the subject. A man missing three fingers on his right hand will have to learn new ways of buttoning a coat and pulling on his boots.

<u>26.</u>

Young Lawrence Wyatt, the physician on call at Gladstone's Good Samaritan Hospital, has been telephoned and summoned, and he arrives at the hospital within a half hour. When he unwraps the blood-soaked towel covering George's hand, the doctor's eyes, heavy-lidded with sleep until that instant, widen in shock. In order to regain his professional demeanor, he brings his face close to George's hand and narrows his eyes. Jesus, the doctor says, what the hell happened?

Somebody chopped them off, George answers.

Dr. Wyatt quickly steps back. He addresses his next question to the nurse, a tall, trim, attractive older woman with tiny maps of varicose veins on her cheeks. Have the police been called, Adeline?

It's Margaret, however, who answers. The sheriff, she says. He's been made aware. And he'll likely be here soon enough.

Once again the doctor directs his question to the nurse. Do I wait?

Adeline shakes her head slowly. You do not.

I believe it would be best, Dr. Wyatt says to Margaret, if you waited outside. In the waiting room.

Margaret makes no move to leave but when George

tells her, Go, she walks numbly out of the brightly lit room, her boot heels echoing on the tile floor.

The doctor, a rusty-haired young man who possesses, incidentally, long delicate fingers, carefully turns George's hand over and examines the back as well as the palm.

An axe, you said? Dr. Wyatt asks.

I didn't, George replies. But no. A hatchet.

Well, he keeps it sharp. This is a very clean cut. You must have held still for it.

Didn't have much choice, George says through gritted teeth.

I didn't mean . . . I'm sorry. Never mind. The doctor steps back. My God. Someone who'd do this . . . barbaric.

To this George says nothing. He has tilted his head back and seems to be concentrating on nothing more than breathing in and breathing out.

I'll give you the choice, Dr. Wyatt says. I can put you under, or I can numb it up and you can stay awake.

I'll stay awake.

But you'll have to keep still.

I'm not going anywhere.

After numbing George's hand, Dr. Wyatt smokes a cigarette and makes certain he has everything he needs near at hand. Once he begins, he works slowly and deliberately, as if he's following a checklist in his mind, and he asks no more questions of George, either about his life generally or about the savagery recently unleashed upon him.

The stumps are cleaned with water and alcohol. Some tissue is debrided. The doctor's comments about a clean cut notwithstanding, a few slivers of bone have to be tweezed from the third finger's pulpy mass. The oozing blood vessels and still-wriggling nerve ends are cauterized. The doctor recruits as much loose skin as he can and stitches the flaps together with a network of black thread. Once the sutures are all tied off and the doctor has finished his work, the nurse gives George two injections, one an antibiotic and the other a tetanus vaccine.

When the entire procedure is over, Margaret is called back into the room. George smiles wanly at her and holds up his bandaged hand. Now I'll be wearing mittens instead of gloves.

Margaret ducks inside his raised arm and kisses him on the forehead, just above the cut he received when he banged into the bed frame. It's a gash that might, under other circumstances, have warranted a few stitches. Tonight it's been covered with two Band-Aids. Margaret repeats the phrase that she uttered over and over again as she drove her husband to the hospital. I'm so sorry, she says.

Enough of that, George replies.

We're going to send him up to one of the wards, Dr. Wyatt says. We want to watch for any sign of infection.

The sheriff show up yet? George asks his wife.

Margaret shakes her head. That could have been a bluff.

Did she strike you as the bluffing kind? No, me neither. I expect he'll wait until morning now.

Again, Dr. Wyatt says, we can call the police. Or the sheriff. We should . . . after all, whoever did this—

—knew what he was doing, says George. He tries to smile but a grimace appears instead. To Margaret he says, I don't want you going back to the motel alone.

I won't be long. But I need to get cleaned up. And get dressed. Margaret smiles shyly at this, as if the doctor and nurse could see what she's wearing under her mackinaw. And I'll pack up the car—

Before she finishes, George shakes his head. No. Not alone.

Nurse Adeline steps forward and puts a hand on Margaret's back. He's right, hon. Whoever did this? You need to stay close.

We know very well who did this, Margaret says angrily.

And you'll need to tell the authorities, Dr. Wyatt says. But the swiftness of his remark makes it clear: *But don't tell us.*

Adeline rubs Margaret's shoulder. Here's what we'll do. I'm going to find a bed someplace where you can lie down. My shift is over in a couple hours, and then you and I can go get your things. To George she says, It'll be light then.

George is pale with exhaustion and pain, and he assents wearily to the nurse's plan. He does this with a tired but adept wave of his bandaged hand, as if he's already learned a use for a hand with three fingers missing.

27

THE EMPTY BED THE NURSE HAS FOUND FOR MARGARET is on the obstetrics ward. Only one newborn is in the hospital's nursery, and the instant he begins to cry he is swaddled, lifted out of his bin, and taken to his mother in a ward down the hall from Margaret. The crying stops almost immediately.

The two o'clock feeding, Margaret says to Adeline.

About three hours late. But yes.

I had twins. And I could never get them on quite the same schedule. I'd get one fed and just about when I was ready to fall asleep the other would wake up.

Me, I had six. In nine years. My milk cow years, I call them. More than a decade of raw nipples. Felt like there wasn't an hour or a day when I didn't have a hungry squalling baby coming at me with an open mouth. But now that they're mostly grown and scattered I don't sleep any better. So I'm always willing to work the night shift.

I always said a woman sleeps different than a man. Mother or not.

We've got a woman down the hall who's in her second day of labor. Think we should go down and tell her to turn back now?

She won't need much persuading, says Margaret. Two days? My God. Have you locked her windows?

Adeline shakes out a hospital gown. You can put this on. And if you like I can take that nightdress of yours straight down to the incinerator.

Margaret looks down at her nightgown. George's blood has dried to the color of mahogany and the largest stains have stiffened the fabric. No, Margaret says. No, I better keep this. A reminder of what I got us into.

Won't your husband's hand be all the reminder you need? And unless you were wielding the hatchet, you need to go a little easy on yourself, my dear.

In his years of ranching, Margaret says, George Blackledge came close to losing an arm to a hay baler. He got kicked by horses and fell off a barn roof and broke his ankle. He almost lost fingers and toes to frostbite. When he was sheriff someone clunked him over the head with a paint can. He survived all that, but following me and one of my crazy ideas turns him into a man with only one good hand? No, easy isn't what I have coming.

Then, to hide her tears from a woman who's seen more of them than sunsets, Margaret turns her back and takes off her nightgown. She bares a body that reveals its years as plainly as yellow leaves reveal a season. The bony protrusions of hip and shoulder blade, the slackening belly and buttocks, the sagging tits that look as though they could never have provided sustenance, the liver spots and sun spots, the wrinkles, the gray hair—here is a body in all its aging frailty, yet it is also a body that only hours earlier was tuned to pleasure. But now it's exposed to a nurse, whereas earlier it was gazed on by a man besotted with desire. Margaret slips her arms inside the hospital gown and then reaches behind to fasten the strings.

Here, Adeline says, I'll get those for you. As she knots Margaret's gown, she says, What I've seen of that husband of yours, he doesn't strike me as a man who goes anywhere but that it's of his own choosing.

You'd be right about that most of the time but not now. Margaret shakes her head. If he'd had his way he'd be sleeping in his own bed right now. With me beside him.

Margaret is the one in the hospital gown, but Adeline sits on the bed. I guess you could tell—Dr. Wyatt didn't want to know too much about what happened to your George. He's looking to move on from Gladstone as soon as possible and figures the less involved he is, the easier it'll be.

From the pocket of her uniform Adeline takes out a pack of Pall Malls with a book of matches tucked inside the cellophane. She offers the pack to Margaret, who says no thank you. Adeline lights a cigarette for herself and finds a small tin ashtray on the windowsill. Now me, the nurse says, picking a shred of tobacco from her lip. I'm not going anywhere. I was born here and I'll die here. I know you're waiting on the sheriff, but if you feel like talking you might tell me who did that to your husband.

We got ourselves tangled up with the Weboy clan.

Adeline makes a clucking sound with her tongue. This would be Blanche and her sons?

And the uncle. Bill.

Tangled up is right. You'd as soon get snarled up in barbed wire as have anything to do with the Weboys. And

what did you folks do to get on the wrong side of Blanche
and those dim-witted boys of hers?

Margaret Blackledge's eyes are red-rimmed and sunken
and her voice bobs and quivers more than ever with her exhaustion, but she tells the nurse the story. How, after their
son's death, they took his widow and son into their home
and tried to make it a place where both would want to live.
How Lorna fell for the first smooth-talking, wavy-haired sonofabitch who came along and married him before another
year of grass had healed over the seams of sod on her husband's grave. How unsuited for motherhood Lorna was and
how Donnie was not just an uncaring but a cruel stepfather.
How they lit out for Montana without a moment's consid-
eration for how attached Margaret and George had become
to that child. How they came to Montana hoping to convince Lorna to let the boy come back to live with them. How
Blanche Weboy wants the boy to remain under her roof . . .

Adeline whistles softly. Over the years I've met any
number of women—girls, I should say—who might like to
unload a kid. Or two or three. But I bet not a one of them
would ever say yes if the offer was put right to her. Just not
something a mother can do. Adeline stabs out her cigarette, stands, and smooths the front of her uniform. She
pulls back the covers on the bed. You'd have been better
off, she says, if you'd have stolen the boy away. Because this
Lorna might not have bothered to come after him.

She pats the sheet in invitation and Margaret climbs into
bed. I know enough about Blanche Weboy, says Margaret, to
know why she wants to hang on to the boy. And it doesn't
have a damn thing to do with how much she favors being

a grandma. Once he crossed over into Montana and came into her house he became a Weboy. One of hers. And she doesn't let go of what she thinks is hers.

You've got her pegged, all right. Adeline pulls the covers over Margaret but then, like a mother who knows when she's still needed, sits down on the edge of the bed. Why his fingers? she asks softly.

Margaret covers her face with her hands. George grabbed a gun, she says, then brings her hands down and shakes her head as if trying to refuse the thought. Not right away. I know when it happened and why. They barged into our cabin and of course George's first impulse was to drive them out. But it wasn't until Bill Weboy put his hands on me—no, no, nothing more than a touch—that George grabbed his gun. And he was too slow. But oh, I don't know. They came in *with* the hatchet so who knows what mayhem they had in mind all along. Then they walked out the door with George's pistol, so you can imagine the tale they'll tell the sheriff.

Adeline sighs. Oh my. No way you could know this, of course, but our Sheriff Munson was Blanche Weboy's beau for a time after her husband passed away. He was in deep enough he was ready to leave his wife for her. But he must have had shortcomings she couldn't get past, because she finally sent him back to his wife. Anyway. Lots of folks think that's the only reason her boys aren't getting arrested every day of their lives. I don't know how much of that's so, but when it comes to men she can cast a spell, that's sure.

What have I done, Margaret says. What *have* I done . . .

Adeline smooths the blankets over Margaret and stands up. You rest. I'll take another look in on your husband right now, but then later today I'll go with you to the motel. I'll stand guard while you pack up.

Just the two of us?

Adeline smiles. What? You don't think a couple of old ladies are a match for the Weboys? Besides, this will be broad daylight. The Weboys won't dare do a thing. They need the dark of night for their dealings.

Thank you . . .

Then, until your husband's ready to travel, you'll stay at our place.

I couldn't. Your husband—

Adeline holds up a hand. Ssh. No argument about it. And Homer won't mind. Of course, *you* might. This arrangement will have you sleeping under a drunkard's roof. Which is what Homer Witt is. But he's the gentle kind. And maybe if he's off to a slow start today, he'll come to the motel with us.

28.

Shortly after noon, Margaret and Adeline begin packing up the Blackledges' car. The two women work under a September sun so bright and warm that the white of Adeline's uniform seems sun-bleached rather than store-bought. It's a day sure to give eastern Montanans the feeling that it might be the last of its kind for a long time to come. They leave the cabin door open, and the prairie smells of sage and sun-heated stones enter and mingle with the aroma of cheap soap and bleached linens.

Then, when the car is packed, Margaret obliterates those odors with a new one. The caustic smell of Pine-Sol reaches almost to the highway as Margaret works on her hands and knees, trying to wash her husband's blood tracks off the floor. She scrubs for almost an hour, yet she can't eliminate all the stains. As long as Cabin Number Eight of the Prairie View Motor Court stands, a few dark burgundy drops and streaks will discolor the linoleum.

Before the women drive off, two more chores need to be done.

First Margaret walks to the motel's office. At the counter is a plump young woman with slightly crossed eyes behind thick glasses, who regards Margaret with suspicion.

Margaret hands over the key to Cabin Number Eight

and an envelope. We're checking out, says Margaret. What I calculate we owe you is in here, along with extra for a towel we took when we had a little emergency. I wrote down our address back in North Dakota if you don't think that's fair.

The young woman seems reluctant to take the envelope but finally does, turning it over in her hand like a summons. The envelope bears the name and address of the Prairie View Motor Court, as does the sheet of stationery inside.

As if she's expecting an argument, Margaret waits for a moment.

Okay, the young woman says, and only then does Margaret walk away.

She stops at the door, however, turns around, and jabs a finger in the young woman's direction. But you tell them, says Margaret, her vibrato rising as if her voice were strung on a too-tight wire, you tell them if they're looking for a dispute, they better be ready to answer for their part in what happened here!

Margaret strides out of the office and back to Cabin Number Eight. She goes inside but not for long. When she comes back out she's carrying something. It's a small makeshift parcel made from drawing up the corners of a handkerchief, a handkerchief of the kind neatly stacked and sold in the men's department of Montgomery Ward. Adeline Witt has been standing by the Hudson, and when Margaret approaches, the nurse reaches into the car and brings out the garden trowel that until two hours ago hung from a nail on the wall of the Witts' garage. She hands the trowel to Margaret, who walks off in the direction of the vacant land behind the cabins. Adeline follows her.

You can wait here, Margaret says over her shoulder. I'll do this.

I'll stand watch.

Ten yards from the shadow of the cabin, in a sunlit patch of ground bare but for a few stones, and just before the line where the tall, tough prairie grasses begin their uninterrupted run to the bluffs and buttes in the distance, Margaret Blackledge drops to her knees. After all her hard work scrubbing the cabin floor you'd think her energies might be flagging, but with the trowel she stabs and digs into that hard-baked square of earth as if doing so were her only commission in this world.

While she digs she talks, and though her words must be directed to the woman who is standing nearby with her back turned to Margaret, nothing Margaret says seems to ask for a response. Her talk isn't punctuated so much by the wobble in her voice as by the grunts of exertion as she fights with the earth to make it give way.

The thing about George Blackledge was, Margaret says, he could not get up to make a speech to save his life. And you might think that that shouldn't be a qualification to be a North Dakota sheriff, but it matters. It just *does*. Ask him a question, yes, he could respond, but his answer would be as short as he could make it. I'd try to tutor him a little, suggest he string out his answers a bit. And bore the hell out of people? he'd say. So when he was running for office, I'd come up with little schemes for him to meet the voters. We'd go to church suppers. To all the high school's sporting events. Just walk around the county fair, I'd tell him, and make yourself available. And smile, I'd say. Would it kill you to smile at folks? Make them think you're happy to see them and not resentful of the time it takes to say good day.

She's dug down to pale clay and there she stops. It's deep enough. Deeper.

And she keeps talking. George always ran with Buck Stinson, the state's attorney, and it was likely Buck who carried George into office. Now, Buck had the opposite problem. He could make a speech at the drop of a hat, but you couldn't get him to stop.

She fills in the little grave and then tamps the dirt down hard with the back of the trowel blade. Because of the pebbles in the dirt, the trowel makes a small ringing sound each time Margaret slaps the earth.

I did a little campaigning myself, she says. It didn't bother me to buttonhole folks on the street and give them the reasons why they should vote for George. George used to tell me that I was the one who should run for office. But it's you I believe in, I said. You. Even if you don't believe in yourself.

She gets stiffly to her feet and begins her search for larger rocks. Nothing smaller than a dinner plate or a saucepan will do, but she doesn't have to range far to find stones of sufficient size and weight. These she places carefully on the packed-down dirt, fitting one on top of another with the care of a stonemason. There, she says, wiping her hands on her dungarees. Even if a dog or a coyote gets the scent, they're not going to be able to move these out of the way.

At some point Adeline Witt had walked away and is now waiting at the car. When Margaret Blackledge comes around the corner of the cabin, she walks with the rapid step of someone determined not to look back. Because there's dirt on her hands, she leaves a dark streak when she wipes her cheek. To Adeline, she says, Let's get the hell out of here.

Neither woman speaks again until they are in the heart of Gladstone, on the street that will take them to the hospital.

Can you believe it? Margaret says, both the quaver and the vivacity returned to her voice. Before the Prairie View Motor Court, I'd never before stayed in a hotel or motel two nights in a row. Even our honeymoon, in the Grand View Hotel in Bismarck, North Dakota, was only the one night.

Margaret shields her eyes from the car windshields and storefront plate glass windows glinting in the afternoon sun. But I suppose that second night at the Prairie View doesn't count as an entire night, does it?

29.

ODORS OF ANTISEPTIC AND FLOOR WAX. THE RATTLE OF bed rails being lifted into place, of clipboards taken from their hooks and put back on again. The hush of rubber-soled shoes, of a wheelchair pushed down a long corridor. The grunt and groan of an old man trying to find ease in his sleep . . . In the hospital ward, Margaret Blackledge sits at her husband's bedside, and she's drawn her chair close enough to hold his unbandaged hand in hers and to be heard as she speaks to him in a voice barely above a whisper. George's eyes are closed, and it's impossible to tell whether he's listening or dozing through her monologue.

You know what I was thinking about today, George? I was remembering when the twins started school, and you and I both drove them into town and watched them walk together into Emerson Elementary. I suppose there's something in the September sunlight that brought all this on . . . Anyway. Do you remember that day? Just before they stepped through the door, James turned around and waved his sad, brave little wave. None of that for Janie, of course. She marched right in like she expected they'd been waiting for her arrival. Then we drove back to the ranch. We looked at each other like we weren't sure what we were supposed to do with all those alone hours. Well, it took us about three seconds to figure that out, didn't it? As if we didn't both have work waiting for us. As I recall, we ended up right there on the floor of the parlor. Just like back when we were both a couple of randy, impatient kids.

Uh-oh, George says, his eyes still closed. If you're whispering in my ear about the happy old days, that can't be a good sign. Didn't you say that was the last thing old Strawberry heard before we put her down?

Oh, don't, George. Don't joke with me. I'm feeling . . . oh, I don't know what I'm feeling. Regretful. Remorseful. All I've brought us to. And the good, good life I took us away from.

Come on now. He opens his eyes and gives her hand a little shake. Don't be one of those people who spruces up the past with her imagination.

Are you saying I'm not remembering that parlor floor right, Mr. Blackledge?

No, I'll testify to that memory.

This conversation takes place during Good Samaritan's afternoon visiting hours, and the Blackledges fall silent when a jaunty man walks into the ward. He's wearing a wide-shouldered, double-breasted brown suit flecked with slubs of lighter-colored fabric, two-tone wing tips, and the type of hat favored by the president. He stops at the foot of George Blackledge's bed and rubs his hands together like a cook who is happily surprised at how the soup has turned out.

Well, well, he says. Can't enjoy the day's favors lying in here, can you?

The beds on either side of George are unoccupied. The only other patient on the ward is an emaciated elderly man in the bed nearest the door. An occasional moan breaks the rhythm of his wheezing breaths.

George says nothing but regards the visitor coolly. Margaret, who remains seated at her husband's bedside, asks, What can we do for you?

The man removes his hat and begins to bow but then only stiffly dips his head. It's I who can do for you.

I who can do for you. The bounce in his step, the barely held-back ebullience—there's something about this man that suggests he, like Lawrence Wyatt, is not from Gladstone, though he is decades older than the young doctor.

Unless you can make fingers grow back, says George, I doubt that.

The man's smile, which has been constant since he entered the ward, grows even wider. Mr. and Mrs. Blackledge, my apologies. I thought my visit had been announced, but plainly you have no idea who I am.

Yet you know us, says Margaret.

Indeed I do. It's my business to do so. I not only know who you are, I know what your business has been in our county. Furthermore, I have something of yours in my possession.

What might that be? George asks the question but his exhaustion is such that he hardly seems to care about the answer.

Sitting on my desk is a .45 caliber automatic that I believe once belonged to you.

You're welcome to it, says George. I hope it brings you better luck than it brought me.

The man draws himself to his full height. You find some humor in this situation?

George holds up his bandaged hand as if in an obscene gesture. You see me laughing?

Margaret puts a restraining hand on her husband's wrist. Just who might you be, sir?

Franklin Reese, Gladstone County attorney. He extends his hand to Margaret, who doesn't take it, and while Mr. Reese could reach out his left hand for George to shake, he doesn't.

A politician, George says.

I've been elected to office. Yes. You know something about that, I gather.

Enough to know it's court business brought you here.

In a manner of speaking.

George pushes himself up on his elbows and raises himself to a sitting position. Then say it.

Mr. Reese drops his hat on the bed near the mound made by George's feet. Very well. I'm as capable of direct speech as you, Mr. Blackledge. The sheriff and I have conferred. Once you're released from the hospital, you're free to go back to your home in Dickinson.

Dalton.

I beg your pardon?

Dalton. We live in Dalton, North Dakota. Not Dickinson. Why was I told Dickinson?

Does this matter? Margaret says, lowering her head and shaking it impatiently. What about Sheriff Munson? We were told to expect a visit from him.

Franklin Reese says, I'm speaking for both of us.

And for the court, George says.

Yes, in a manner of speaking.

The point you're trying to make, George says, is that

I'm free to go wherever. Dickinson or Dalton. Which is a chickenshit way of saying that the son of a bitch who took a hatchet to my hand can also go wherever he pleases.

As with all cases, different sides have different stories to tell.

George shifts in his bed, and Franklin Reese's hat slides to the floor. The attorney promptly picks it up. And you, George says to the attorney, don't want to bother sorting them out. Even though it's your goddamn job to do exactly that.

Give a man a hat and you increase his confidence and put him at ease. Now he can turn the hat in his hands, adjust its crease or brim, run his fingers around the band. I would suggest, the attorney says, continuing to smile, that you accept what is being offered to you. He widens his smile and addresses Margaret. Accept it and go. He puts on his hat and only then does his smile diminish. No need to thank me.

Attorney Reese performs his rigid little bow again and walks away. When he passes a nurse in the doorway, he touches the brim of his hat.

Adeline Witt has been watching the county attorney since he entered the ward, and now she walks out behind him.

George sinks back into his pillow and closes his eyes. I should have spotted him for a politician right from the get-go. Him and his goddamn smile.

Politicians and Indian boys, says Margaret. Young Mr. Dragswolf never stopped smiling either.

A few of those Weboys were smilers too. And the uncle, sure as hell. And now we know why.

Maybe, Margaret says, folks in this part of the world are just so damn happy to be here they can't stop smiling.

George's eyes remain closed though there is no movement under the lids. Beneath all the hospital's other odors is a smell both sweet and sulfuric. It's the odor that accompanies unconsciousness and release from pain. Ether. After a long silence, George says, Maybe.

And now we've had our visit from the sheriff. In a manner of speaking.

He about wore that out, didn't he?

What I can't figure, she says, is that everywhere we go, people seem in agreement about what no-good troublesome bastards the Weboys are. Yet here it is—excuses made for them. And they're out there and we're in here.

Bastards they may be, but they're *their* bastards. He opens his eyes and slowly turns his gaze to Margaret. And this isn't jail. You can walk out of here anytime you like.

Don't, George.

For that matter, you could have walked out of Jack Nevelsen's jail. You're as free now as you've ever been.

I'm right where I want to be. And I've been thinking, George. About the life we'll go back to. I'm so sorry I didn't give more careful thought to what I wanted—to what I thought I wanted. You're right, of course. A child running around the house—I don't have the energy for that. I like my routines. We both do. We're too old and stuck in our ways to start bending our schedules for a little boy's life.

So you're ready to give up, then, are you? asks George. That's not like you. That's not a goddamn bit like the Margaret Blackledge I've been trying to keep up with for forty years.

Well, maybe we were both wrong about who she is, George.

In reply, George pushes himself up on his elbows once again, a maneuver that he performs with more effort than when Franklin Reese was standing over the bed. He reaches across to his wife and with his bandaged hand paws at and then presses against her breast.

Margaret doesn't lift his hand away or shift out of his reach. She doesn't look around the ward to determine who might be witnessing her husband's behavior. She leans into his touch, but gently. Neither of them can be sure yet of what his hand can and cannot bear.

But in its deliberation, George's gesture has nothing to do with intimacy or desire. George Blackledge is satisfying a curiosity; he is assaying the world in which he will live.

Then he falls back on his pillow and shuts his eyes again.

30.

WHEN VISITING HOURS ARE OVER, MARGARET Blackledge walks out into the sunlight and the heat that feels more like August than the end of September. How will she fill the hours until she can return to her husband's side? A meal for which she has no appetite? Aimless wandering of Gladstone's streets? She turns a slow, indecisive circle.

And there they are. Looking like mother and daughter on a shopping excursion. Or as though they had a meeting with the minister to discuss the plans for a wedding. Or a funeral. In their Sunday dresses, Blanche and Lorna step out of the building's shadow where they've been waiting.

They come forward and though you can be certain she doesn't mean to, Margaret takes a step back.

Now don't scamper off, says Blanche.

You've got your nerve. Showing up here.

Blanche Weboy smiles an unapologetic smile. We wanted to pay a visit to the ward. But your guardian Mrs. Witt advised against it. Advised very strongly, I should say.

We came to see, Lorna says softly, how Grandpa George is.

And did she—Margaret jabs her finger in Blanche's direction—tell you how he came to be in his condition?

Lorna nods meekly.

And you can allow yourself to be seen in her company?

Lorna asks, Will he be all right?

He doesn't think so. But yes.

Blanche unclasps her purse and gropes through its interior.

Don't tell me—you're about to pull a hatchet out of there.

Blanche only smiles and continues her search. In another moment she pulls out a tissue and waves it daintily in the air. Truce?

I'd as soon make peace with a rattlesnake.

Blanche Weboy stops waving the tissue but keeps it poised in the air. Listen to you.

On the oaks and elms hovering over the hospital, enough leaves remain to dapple these women in the afternoon sun.

Lorna looks up and down the street as if she's hoping someone will come along and take her away. But with a single question Margaret jerks her back to this sunny square of sidewalk. Where's Jimmy?

Back at the house.

When *do* you spend time with him?

As if this is the purpose she had planned for the tissue all along, Blanche wipes her nose. Still telling people how to run their lives, she says. Some folks never learn.

Am I supposed to learn from you? You haven't got a damn thing to teach me, unless it's how to act like a savage.

You're scaring Lorna, Blanche says calmly. She stuffs the Kleenex back in her purse and clasps it. She scowls at Margaret. But you better make peace with me, missus, if you want to see your grandson again.

Margaret, who had been on the point of walking away, now must stand in place and do nothing while Blanche Weboy says and does what she will. The effort at stillness trembles Margaret.

And it is Blanche who walks away, taking Lorna with her. But they don't go far. Blanche stops abruptly and returns. She steps up so close to Margaret there's barely room for sunlight to come between them. The hell of it is, says Blanche, if we were each on the other's side of the Badlands, we'd probably do exactly what the other's doing.

· · ·

George opens his eyes to find Adeline Witt standing over him with her arms crossed and a cheerless expression on her face.

Before he can speak, she asks, What can I do for you? Force a man to express his desire before he's ready and you have him at a disadvantage.

Bring me my pants.

Now, if I did that, you'd likely walk out of here.

That's the idea.

The doctor isn't ready to cut you loose.

Waiting to see if my fingers will grow back, is he?

She smiles at him, exposing a few gold-backed teeth in the process, but the effort seems to cost her. I heard you try out that line on Mr. Reese. I know your kind, Mr. Blackledge. You're so damn good at accepting the harsh realities that you use it to bully other folks. But doctor's orders or no, I might be tempted to bring you your trousers if I thought you'd pull them on and then you and your missus head right back to North Dakota. What say you? Any chance of that?

Can I tell you a little story, Mrs. Witt?

Adeline. But fire away.

This was shortly after I was sworn in as sheriff. I'd been hearing about a young fellow name of Norman Rugda. Now, Norman grew up on a dirt-poor farm in the southeast corner of the county, and maybe because of that, when he moved to Dalton he couldn't keep his hands off other people's goods. Never anything we could prove, however. Then one day someone charged into my office shouting that Norman had just stolen his shotgun, stole it from this fellow's car, and in broad daylight. Just as I was walking out of the office to investigate, I saw Norman drive past in his old truck. Well, I climbed into the squad car and gave chase, as they say. Once Norman knew I was behind him, he took off into the hills west of Dalton. This was a regular high-speed pursuit, my first, and on a steep dirt road I watched Norman almost lose control when his old truck hit a washout at the bottom of the hill. Quick as you please, I did the adding and subtracting: no shotgun was worth my life. Or Norman's. Especially since Norman was almost certain to return to Dalton within a week at most. Which is exactly what he did, and he came back boasting that he had outrun the sheriff. When I caught wind of that, I grabbed myself a tire iron and walked up behind Norman Rugda in the Roundup Bar, where he was holding forth, and walloped him across the back of his knees. He folded like a broken sunflower stalk. Later, when Norman was serving his sentence in the county jail, he'd call me to his cell periodically so I could witness the changing colors of the bruises on the back of his legs.

George raises himself in the hospital bed, a maneuver

he has now become adept at performing. He holds up his good hand. Now, he says, before you think I'm nothing but another old mossback who can't stop talking about his buckaroo days, let me get to the point. When I was following Bill Weboy out to the ranch, it felt a little like I was racing after Norman Rugda. But when I did the arithmetic this time, I came up with a different sum. The law be damned and caution go to hell. That was Margaret Blackledge in the car ahead of me. I was ready to drive off the end of the earth if need be.

Is that the point you were getting to, Mr. Blackledge? Or are you just going the long way around to persuade me to bring you your trousers?

What I'm saying is, my wife's alone out there in a world full of Weboys. I'd like to be by her side, whether she wants to head back home or try to visit her grandson again.

For a long moment Adeline Witt stares down at George Blackledge, who, for all his white-whiskered pallor, his missing fingers, and muscles rusting from age and disuse, still has eyes that burn with a wild, blue desperation.

The nurse bends over, lifts his bandaged hand, and examines the underside of his arm. The doctor's concerned about sepsis, she says. Blood poisoning, to you. So no pants for you, Mr. Blackledge. Not for another day or two. Anything else you need?

In that case, you could fetch me a bottle of whiskey. And pull the cork for me.

31.

ON THE NARROW FRONT PORCH THE TWO WOMEN SIT. Coffee cups steam near at hand. The porch light is off and no illumination from the house finds its way out here. Only a streetlamp breaks up the darkness, and its glow is hemmed in by the leaves of the maples and elms that spread out over this city street. The end of September, yet the women's arms are bare.

You haven't had a frost yet? asks Margaret.

You should ask Homer, says Adeline. Since he had to quit both the filling station and the volunteer fire department, he's got nothing better to do than keep records of such things. Working nights, I sometimes even lose track of the seasons.

Crickets. The reason I asked. You don't generally hear crickets after a frost.

Adeline cocks her head. You don't say. Well, they're chirping away now, aren't they.

The night before we left, says Margaret, we had a hard freeze. I knew it was coming but I didn't bother covering anything up. We were leaving—well, I knew *I* was leaving—and I wasn't sure when I'd be back so the hell with it, I said. Why bother? And you know, it felt damn good. Now I'm not sure if I'll ever bother covering a tomato plant or my asters or mums again.

You mean to say you didn't know he'd follow you? I find that hard to believe.

When the women shift in their chairs, the wicker under them creaks and harmonizes with the crickets' song.

I suppose I knew, Margaret says.

I've been around the man for less than a day and I could have made that prediction.

Yes, I knew. I knew.

They drink their coffee. Somewhere on the block a car grumbles along in a low gear. A screen door slams. Those crickets. Summer sounds, out of season.

Margaret crosses her arms, then brings her hand up to provide a steadying brace for her chin. You saw what we'd packed in the car—I'd loaded up damn near everything in the house. Everything we'd need to live out of the car for months, if need be. And that was the vision I had— George and me on the road, chasing Donnie, Lorna, and Jimmy, traipsing all over the West. We'd have ourselves a real adventure. By the time we caught up to them we'd have *earned* Jimmy, as if there is such a thing . . . Yes, I figured they'd run and run. What could I have been thinking? People go home. Simple as that. Hard times come or they need a helping hand, they go home. It's what George and I did after we were married. No, that's not exactly right. We didn't *go* back. We never left. We stayed on the ranch, helping out at first. Then running the outfit when Dad got too old to climb on a horse. By that time the place was all but ours. And then when my mother passed away, it was. Ours, I mean. Title and deed. So why didn't I figure right with

Donnie? We found him the second place we looked, and that first wrong turn wasn't that far off . . . and now here we are. A hell of an adventure! No, when George bought himself a pint of bourbon before we left town, it wasn't so he could deal with all those days and weeks on the road. He bought it so he could abide all the stubborn, foolish decisions his wife was making. Making for both of us . . .

Well hell, I might as well come out with it, Adeline says, clapping her hand against her thigh. I might be adding to the problem. I bought a bottle of whiskey and took it in to your husband.

Margaret finally lifts her trembling chin from her palm. Well, you're the nurse.

And I poured him a glass. Then I put the cap back on and put the bottle away. But when you pack him up to go, be sure to check in the drawer of the little cabinet next to the bed.

You're the nurse, Margaret says again. You wouldn't have done it if you didn't think it would do him some good.

Hell, I don't think it does anybody any *good*. But I suppose I thought it wouldn't do him any great harm. Unless I misjudged the man, I'm guessing he knows how to keep it under control. Like my Homer in there. Who's in and out of his bottle all day long. But he's never more than a little drunk. Of course he's never more than a little sober, either.

Well, it got away from George for a while. He scared himself bad enough that he swore off it altogether.

Was this when you lost your son?

Before. George handled James's death the way he'd handle a sickness. Wrapped up tight inside himself and waited for the misery to pass. Margaret pauses and clears her throat. No, his drinking got out of hand a few years earlier. And you're right: he was like your husband. A little drunk twenty-four hours a day. He was sheriff then, and I said to him, What do you suppose happens when someone smells whiskey on your breath? Don't you imagine that's one less vote? And he'd say what he always said about elections: They're free to vote for who they like. God, getting that man to court a vote was like pulling hens' teeth. So he kept drinking. I had the feeling he was trying to shut something off that wouldn't stop any other way, some memory or feeling. Or maybe something he saw on the job. Whatever it was—if there even was an it—he wouldn't talk to me about it. And then he up and quit drinking. I didn't notice right away, which I suppose was a good sign. When I finally said something to him on the subject, he said, Oh, I quit that a couple months back. Just like he didn't tell me he started up again.

The best I can get out of Homer, says Adeline, is that he likes the taste.

Which I have trouble believing.

Margaret rises and walks to the porch railing, grips it tight, then pushes and pulls herself back and forth a few times. But I could never get him to understand what it was about Jimmy and me, either. George said to me, You have to let him go someday. What does it matter whether it's now or a few years from now? That's what we raise them for, to go. And I couldn't argue with him. I knew he was right. I knew. And the knowing didn't make a damn bit of difference.

It's not the same, says Adeline, with women and men. That's what she says, but in her voice is more politeness than conviction.

Thank you, says Margaret. Thank you for that.

Though I have to say, Adeline continues, I'm with your husband on this one. The letting-go business. Of course, I never had a child taken from me before I was ready to say good-bye. Hell, I worry they're going to come back. And stay.

The day Lorna took Jimmy away I was scurrying around the house. Trying to find all his toys and things to pack up. I suppose someone might have believed I was eager for him to go. But keeping busy is my way when I can't . . . when it's . . .

Am I remembering right? Adeline asks. You had twins? One of each? How about your daughter? What's her situation?

Living in Minneapolis. Working for a company that provides some kind of financial service for farmers, though as near as George and I can tell, nobody in the company ever sets foot on a farm. Janie's given up on us ever understanding what she does for a living. But that's not what you're asking, is it? No, she doesn't have a husband. Or kids.

Not that one child can ever replace another.

Not that they ever can . . . but the ways they resemble each other . . . Did you ever notice, I'm sure you did, how different it feels to pick up and hold different children? Apart from their size, I mean? There wasn't more than an ounce or two's difference in the twins' weight when they were born, and they stayed close until they were nine or ten. But when I picked up James, it was like his weight was distributed differently or something. He'd come up so easily and then arrange himself just right in your arms. I could have hauled him around all day. But Janie—my God. It was like she found a way to turn heavier as soon as you tried to lift her. And she'd squirm and buck in your arms. Then, when Jimmy was born, one of the first things I noticed was how effortlessly he came up into my arms. Like feathers. Like his father . . .

Margaret pivots sharply back to the street. And your children? she asks. Six of them, did you say? She looks up and down the street as if Adeline's children could emerge from the warm haze of this autumn night. But none live here, you said?

Missoula's the closest. And in his case, that's plenty close enough.

The women fall silent again. But the crickets keep on chirping a tune as if they were waiting for the singers to resume. Then Margaret turns to face her friend again, though she keeps her hold on the porch rail. Before long Margaret speaks, and as she does the true source of her voice's tremolo seems finally revealed, the quaver a result of holding too tightly to these words and for too long a time.

Oh hell, she says, I might as well get this out. George has got it in his head I was unfaithful to him.

There are too many questions Adeline could ask, but probably none would be the right one, so she says nothing and waits for Margaret to continue.

This was—my God, closing in on thirty years ago. We were living on the ranch, and the twins weren't much older than Jimmy is now. George was in his first term and one night he saw something—or thought he saw something— that gave him a notion he's carried with him ever since.

We had a little creek running through our place.

Alphabet Creek, we called it, and it watered our stock, and the neighbors' too, specifically the Hildebrands'. They had a son, Robert, and Robert and I practically grew up together. Our mothers bathed us in the same galvanized tub, and when it was time to start school the two of us trekked off to Winship School, a one-room country school, first grade through eighth, about a mile from our ranch. During the winter we'd walk to and from school by following a fence-line, and when I say *following* I mean there were a few blizzards when one of us had to keep a hand on the wire every step of the way. High school, we saddled up and rode horseback to Dalton—the cowboy and the cowgirl, some of the town boys called us.

Anyway, the year I'm talking about, we had a summer about as hot and parched as any that region ever knew. Day after day of bright blue skies and the sun beating down on us like a hammer. The earth got so damn dry it cracked like a dinner plate. But hot as it was, Alphabet Creek was still running, and not far from the house there was a little oxbow, and right there where the creek curled we had water a little deeper, maybe waist-high at its deepest.

One night I wandered out there late. The twins were sleeping, but I couldn't, not in that heat. I can handle the cold, but hot weather does me in. Always has. Puts me on edge and wears me out both.

It was a full moon, or nearly so, and I was out by the creek, the water flashing gold in the moonlight. George used to take turns with his deputy working night shifts. I'd say, You're the sheriff. You don't have to work nights. You can order your deputy to do that job. Or let it go. Anyone needing a sheriff at three o'clock in the morning knows how to find you. But he wouldn't hear of it. Said his deputy had a wife and family too, so it wouldn't be right to have him working every night.

There I go, straying from the subject again. But getting old is like climbing up to a great height, and when you look down, all the paths intertwine. You can't go down one but that sooner or later it's connected to another.

So there I am, down by the creek on a moonlit night that's so damn hot the rocks underfoot still hadn't cooled down from the day's sun.

I couldn't help myself. I waded into the cool water, and once I was in up to my ankles I knew what I was going to do.

Soon I was splashing around out there, giddy because I'd finally figured out what to do about the heat. It occurred to me that maybe I should go get the twins and bring them down to the creek too, but if they could sleep, why would I disturb that?

Anyway, on that sweltering night who should show up down at the creek but Robert? Seems he'd discovered it as a way to beat the heat long before I did.

Now Robert, he didn't have the most fortunate of lives. He worked the family ranch, same as George and I did, but his father would not sign the place over to him. And old Mr. Hildebrand held on into his nineties, rotting away in a dark back bedroom, but by God not giving in. And then Robert married a sickly woman, so he had all the ranch duties, plus a wife and a father who needed nursing. I suppose it shouldn't have come as any surprise that he was down at the creek in the middle of the night—when the hell else would he have a moment for himself?

So there we both were, Robert and me, and pretty soon we're whooping it up like the kids we once were. Skinny-dipping, I guess is the name for it. Abruptly Margaret stops her story and looks closely at her friend. Margaret's waiting, but for what? Encouragement? Understanding? Forgiveness?

But from Adeline Witt comes only this impassive remark: It's not for me to say what it was.

And for another moment, Margaret remains silent, poised between going on and turning back. She goes on, as anyone who has known her for as little as an hour knows she would.

That's what it was then. Whatever you'd call it. The two of us naked as when we were babes in the washtub. But I knew it was a grown-up thing to Robert. I could see that. But hell, we were alone out there on private property at two o'clock in the morning. Two people who'd found a little relief from the heat and maybe the drudgery of their lives, too. Going back to easier, younger days.

Except we weren't so alone.

George had been called out that night, a fatal car accident on one of the county roads, and on his way back to the office he decided to stop by the ranch. That was not a usual thing for him. If he was on duty, he was on duty. But the accident was car-train, and there's nothing more gruesome than that, and it must have shaken him. He knew the young fellow who was killed—Myron Berkshaw. Though it wouldn't have been like him, maybe George was putting off the worst part of his job: knocking on a door and handing over the hard news that a loved one is dead. Maybe he wanted to look in on his own kids. Or maybe he just wanted a cup of coffee. I never knew, because George never came any closer than that hill road that looked down on the ranch and on Alphabet Creek . . .

But he never mentioned to me that he saw Robert and me cooling off in the middle of the night. That wasn't the George Blackledge way. Oh no. He'd figure if I was out there naked in the world with another man it was somehow his own fault. That was George. Still is. Take it all on himself. It was Robert who told me George had seen us. George didn't say a word for years, and then one day he drove up to the Hildebrands' place, knocked on the door, and when Robert answered, George grabbed him by the throat and told Robert that if he had designs on me he should come right out and say so instead of sneaking around our place in the middle of the night. Designs! Can you imagine? But that too was George Blackledge. Keep a thing closed up tight inside yourself and let its acid eat away at you. Make yourself miserable with anger and jealousy, but don't say anything to get the matter out in the open. Robert and I, who as I say had been my friend from childhood, had only one more conversation, and that was so Robert could report to me what my husband had seen, said, and done.

Then it was up to me to speak to George about what happened that night. Nothing, I told him. Not a damn thing. A couple old friends splashing around on a hot night. Acting foolish. All right, George said. If you say so. And then he walked away. No argument. No accusation. Hell, if I'd asked him to forgive me, he'd have done it in a minute.

But, Adeline says, I'm guessing you never asked.

What was I supposed to do—ask him to forgive me for what never happened? For what he imagined?

For a long moment this question hangs in the warm night air.

Somewhere in the neighborhood someone is burning leaves. Only where there are lawns are leaves gathered or dispersed or burned by something other than wind and decay, and the smoke from this fire drifts down the street as little more than a haze, the tannic odor as much a part of the season as the sight of trees unburdening themselves.

Finally Adeline says, You're asking me about matters that aren't for me to answer. Then Adeline pushes herself out of her chair and takes the two long steps that bring her alongside her friend. But I don't suppose, Adeline continues, there's anything you can say now that will keep him from seeing that sight in his mind. That's a hard thing for a man.

Margaret turns once again, leaning over the railing as though she were looking over a precipice. You're friend enough to me, she says, that I'll say something to you that I'd never say to another human being: if I never hear again about what's hard for a man, it'll be too goddamn soon.

Though Margaret can't see this, Adeline nods in agreement.

32.

MARGARET LEANS FARTHER OUT FROM THE PORCH. Someone is coming down the walk. And in the same instant she notices a car driving slowly down the street—a blue Ford. Bill Weboy drives a blue Ford! But the man strolling down the sidewalk—is this possible?

The man stops in front of the Witt home, and the car speeds away. Good evening, ladies, says Bill Weboy. Feels more like July than September, doesn't it?

The smoke from his cigar drifts toward the porch and Margaret staggers back as suddenly as if its odor signaled the presence of a poisonous gas. Adeline rises from her chair and stands behind Margaret, ready, it seems, to halt Margaret's retreat or to prop her up if that becomes necessary.

Bill Weboy smiles like a man who remembers every joke he's ever heard. His head of luxuriant hair looks freshly combed. His cheeks and chin glisten as a man's do when he's just shaved. His powerful chest makes his white shirt look like a billowing sail, and when he walks forward and places one booted foot on the bottom porch step, he seems as though he could overwhelm these women with nothing but his confidence and his vigor. But when you've spent hours inside a hospital's walls, everyone on the outside can seem preternaturally healthy.

That's close enough, says Adeline.

With an exaggerated motion Bill Weboy removes his boot from the porch step. I tried to pay a call on your husband, Mrs. Blackledge, but when I arrived at the hospital, visiting hours were over.

If you'd tried to come into his room while I was there, says Margaret, I'd have blocked the door myself.

By God, it's getting so a man can't even shake another's hand and say no hard feelings.

For you, sir, I have nothing but feelings hard as granite.

Bill Weboy laughs, a sound like windswept leaves. Mrs. Blackledge, you can spar with the best of them!

The front door opens and a short, balding, bandy-legged man steps onto the porch. He's wearing moccasins, dungarees held up by suspenders, and a flannel shirt.

Jesus Christ, he says in a soft, high-pitched voice. How come you Weboys keep showing up where you're not wanted?

Hello, Homer, says Bill Weboy. How be you? And to answer your question, how the hell are we supposed to know we're not wanted until we show up?

In your case, Adeline says, you could just assume.

Bill Weboy drags deeply on his cigar and then, in a voice that pretends to confidentiality, says to Margaret, One thing about Gladstone. It's not the most neighborly town.

But Margaret's attention is elsewhere. Bill Weboy's Ford is coming slowly down the street again and staying close to the curb. The car's pale blue has turned to gray in the darkness.

Homer Witt sees it too. Who's that behind the wheel? One of your half-wit nephews?

Homer, I had no idea you kept such close track of the Weboys.

Or did you think you'd better bring the whole family to help you handle these ladies?

Give me a minute here, Homer. Bill Weboy exhales cigar smoke toward the night sky. I'm biting my tongue to keep from saying something about the day when I can't handle two ladies . . . and them grateful to be handled.

Homer Witt says, By God, and starts toward the porch steps. His wife steps in front of him in a nimble maneuver that could be performed only by someone who has years of practice herding the man without his awareness. She is half a head taller than her husband.

Adeline says, My husband here is fool enough to think that if he comes down off this porch, the two of you could settle matters fair and square. He doesn't know he'd be up against your whole goddamn clan in no time. And who knows what they'd bring in the way of knives or hatchets or clubs?

He's the one started with the insults—

But me, I don't give a damn about what's fair. Not when it comes to you and yours. Which is why I'm ready to step inside the door and grab the shotgun out of the hall closet and come out here and open up on you and that carload of nephews or whoever the hell you brought with you.

Bill Weboy raises his hands in mock surrender and takes a step back. Mrs. Witt! You surprise me! And you someone who's sworn to help the sick and injured!

You sonofabitch, Homer says, his soft voice rising even higher.

The Ford has stopped in front of the Witt home. Inside

the car three dark heads are turned dumbly in the same direction, as if the porch and its yellow light were what attracted them and not the figures ranged there in a tableau of opposition.

Bill Weboy says, Good to see you're as red-hot and ready to scuffle as ever, Homer. Folks have said that heart attack slowed you to a crawl. But I can report, not so, not so at all. Homer is still Homer. He's just not a fixture at the Elks like he used to be.

At idle, the Ford's engine has smoothed out and thrums evenly. The car's headlights illuminate the back of the Blackledges' Hudson, the numerals of their North Dakota license plate—133-407—blackly gleaming.

Margaret says, You have to leave these good people alone, Mr. Weboy. Please.

These would be the good people threatening to beat the hell out of me or blow me to kingdom come?

From somewhere on the block comes the hollow, rubbery *ponk* of a kicked ball, followed by a shout—*Hah! No good!* It's late for boys to be playing football. Good weather or not, it's still a school night.

Please, Margaret says again.

Here you're asking me to leave, Mrs. Blackledge, and I only came here to smoke the peace pipe. You have to believe me when I say how sorry I am your visit here turned out the way it did. Even if the only reason you came here was to talk a mother out of her only child. No, no, let me finish. I'm here to see if you can use any help with anything. I know you got yourself checked out of the Prairie View okay. And you and Adeline got your car packed and ready to go. So it seems like you took care of everything on your own. You said good-bye to Blanche and Lorna. And whatever farewell you gave that grandson will have to be good enough. Bill Weboy turns away from the porch, takes two steps, and throws his cigar as hard and as high as he can. It tumbles end over end, its sparks pinwheeling through the dark. When he faces Margaret and the Witts once again, it is without any pretense of courtesy or charm. When that husband of yours gets out of the hospital? Get the hell out of Gladstone. I mean it. Don't dawdle.

Bill Weboy's business is done. He doesn't stroll down the sidewalk as he did when he approached the Witt home. He strides across the lawn and climbs into the waiting automobile.

As soon as the Ford pulls away, a football bounces erratically into the street in front of the Witts' house. It must be the ball that one of the boys kicked moments before, but no one runs into the street after it. When it finally wobbles to rest against the curb it's with a stillness so complete it seems the ball will remain there forever. Where is the boy whose heart will break if he can't find his football? Where is the boy who will be punished if he loses the football he once begged for? But the crickets' scraping song has nothing to say on the subject of boys and their playthings.

33.

GEORGE BLACKLEDGE SITS ON THE EDGE OF HIS BED WITH the bottle held tight between his thighs. It's two o'clock in the morning. The ward is dark and the only sound is the stertorous breathing of the old man four beds away from George. With the fingers of his left hand, George tries to take the cap off the bottle of Old Crow.

His first attempts are clumsy and unnatural, but eventually he's able to coordinate the twisting and pulling. Whiskey fumes rise from the open bottle. Good enough. Then, with less effort than he expended earlier, he puts the cap back on and returns the bottle to the cabinet.

As he does, a figure walks out of the shadows and approaches his bed.

In a voice pitched perfectly between speech and whisper, as only someone practiced in a hospital's middle-of-the-night hush can manage, Adeline Witt says, That's a hell of a lot of work to go through and then not even bring the bottle to your lips.

Just checking to see if I could do it, says George. In case of an emergency.

And awake at two o'clock in the morning doesn't qualify?

You tell me. I didn't think you were on duty tonight.

I'm not. But I've got so I can't sleep unless the sun's up. I thought I'd come look in on the customers.

George stares at her a long moment, longer than he needs to, in the dim light of the ward. I should have noticed, he says, you're not wearing the uniform. Then he leans to the side in order to look past her and into the corridor. Is Margaret out there?

She's sleeping in our spare room. She needs the rest. I sneaked out past her.

Well, you accomplished what our kids could never do.

Adeline Witt has pulled on a cardigan sweater over the sleeveless dress she was wearing earlier in the evening. Temperature's dropping, she says. I guess our warm weather was too good to last.

It never does.

Adeline steps closer to the bed. How's that hand tonight? Keeping you awake?

No more than the grunting and groaning coming from the old gentleman over there. He might be sound asleep, but he sounds like he's hard at work.

Hard at work he is, says Adeline. That's Mr. Amos Banter. Ninety-four years old. Amos says he can remember when soldiers came home from the Civil War. I doubt old Amos will leave this building under his own power.

So, are his efforts to stay in this world or get out of it?

That you would even ask that question, Mr. Blackledge, says a hell of a lot about your character. Now scooch over, she says, and let's bring that bottle back out. I need a little whiskey heat before I head out in the cold.

The bed is narrow and its rail is up on one side. George Blackledge doesn't have much room to maneuver and accommodate Adeline Witt's request. Or does his reluctance have less to do with the bed's confines and more to do with the fact that since he married Margaret Mann, no females but his wife and daughter have dented a mattress at his side?

But the way Adeline eases herself onto the bed has nothing to do with intimacy and everything to do with fatigue. This is a woman whose feet ache at two o'clock in the morning and at two o'clock in the afternoon, and to sit here, closer to George's knees than his shoulder, saves her the steps required to walk around the bed to the chair on the other side.

It is Adeline who brings the bottle of Old Crow out of the cabinet. A water glass, half full, rests on the top of the cabinet, and she pours a little whiskey into the glass and drinks off water and whiskey without pause. She holds the bottle out toward George and sloshes the liquid back and forth. Still not an emergency for you? she asks.

Not yet.

She puts the bottle away and says, I wouldn't be wrong, would I, Mr. Blackledge, if I marked you for a man who likes to get right up close to temptation and then step back?

He says nothing.

Adeline leans toward George, and with a tender practiced motion she lifts his injured hand. How's that bandage doing? You haven't sprung a leak, have you?

Why do I think, he says, that you came here for some reason other than to look at my bandages?

She brings her face close to his hand as if she needs to engage a sense other than sight—smell, perhaps, or taste—to diagnose this man's condition. If the hand's bothering you, she says, I can get you something for the pain.

You didn't answer my question.

Adeline stares into the empty glass, tilting and rotating it in her hand. She brings the glass to her lips and holds it there long enough for any drop of water and whiskey to slide into her mouth. The taciturnity of these people . . . silence held for so long it becomes almost a material thing, its weight increasing until finally it cannot be borne . . .

Then Adeline says, I like your wife.

All right.

I like her but I don't understand her. Now, maybe that's my failing. When it comes to grandchildren, I'm more afraid that one will be unloaded on me than I am of never seeing one again. To go to the lengths she's willing to go to—

You're not Margaret Blackledge.

No, sir, I'm not. And I wouldn't want to see something happen to her.

George sits up straighter. What's that supposed to mean?

Adeline takes another look into the glass before putting it down. She's treating herself pretty rough over what happened to you. It's all her fault, to hear her say it. You could go easy on her.

That's your advice, is it?

I know. It didn't come asked for. Adeline stands and snugs that cardigan tighter on her bare shoulders. Sometimes, she says, the patient has an easier time of it than the one standing at the bedside.

Does that apply to Mr. Banter over there?

Amos is going it alone.

George Blackledge nods. Something to be said for that.

Somewhere a distant telephone rings, and though its answer is not the responsibility of either of these people, they wait and listen. After two rings the imagination provides

LET HIM GO | 205

reasons for the call. My little girl has the croup . . . My husband's stomach ache is getting so bad he can't hardly stand it . . . After three rings the sound seems to come closer . . . The fever, the pain, the spots of blood . . . Four rings . . . Can I give her something? Anything? Five rings, six . . . Can you send an ambulance? The ringing stops, and George and Adeline breathe easier.

But perhaps the sound of that telephone has brought Adeline back to her profession. She presses the back of her hand to George's forehead. I believe you have a fever. Did they give you something for that?

I'm fine, he says and leans away from her touch.

As long as you can get that bottle open on your own, I suppose you are. Good night, Mr. Blackledge. Get some sleep if you can. I'll see you tomorrow. Or later today, I should say.

Not only did Adeline Witt not wear her white nurse's uniform for this middle-of-the-night visit, she didn't wear the rubber-soled white shoes she wore earlier in the day. George can hear her leather heels *tock-tock*ing all the way down the hall. It's a sound he didn't hear when she approached, but then the human ear is tuned differently for departures than arrivals, as anyone who listens to train whistles knows.

34.

BOTH GEORGE AND HOMER SAY NO TO THE OFFER OF A drink.

Oh come now, says Adeline. You both know you want one. Let's not put on airs.

Fine, Homer says, as if he's only grudgingly giving in to another's argument. But more water than usual.

Mr. Blackledge?

George waves her off again.

I hate to drink alone, says Homer. I'll do it but I hate to.

Don't wait on me, George says.

The men are sitting at a table in the Witts' dining room, while their wives move back and forth from the kitchen, finishing the preparations for lunch.

The meal set out is by and for people whose only confident judgment about food is based on its quantity. Accordingly, on the table are both bread-and-butter and dill pickles, carrot and celery sticks, and sliced tomatoes—the last of the season; slices of jellied roast beef and summer sausage, a block of yellow cheese, cottage cheese, and hard-boiled eggs; soda crackers, slices of white bread, and butter; glasses of cold milk. On the stove a saucepan of vegetable soup simmers; a pot of fresh coffee percolates; in the refrigerator tapioca pudding cools until it's time for dessert; on the cupboard a box of gingersnaps waits to be set out with the coffee. The good silver. Cloth napkins.

You didn't have to go to all this fuss, Margaret says to Adeline. And on your day off.

You'd do the same if Homer and I were in your town.

Would I? I hope so but I don't know . . . I hardly dare be sure of any of the things I once believed.

Adeline waves a dish towel in the air as if to ward off this line of foolish talk. I wish you'd reconsider, she says, and spend another night here before you head for home.

It's kind of you to offer, but George says he needs to sleep in his own bed.

He still looks peaked, if you ask me.

Margaret steps close to Adeline and says softly, If those Weboys were looking for a way to take all the air out of him, they sure as hell succeeded. I've never seen him like this. And this is a man who's pushed his way past some hard moments in his life. But now he seems off somewhere on his own, and he can't see or hear the rest of us.

Adeline nods in understanding. He's trying to work out how he's going to keep on being the man he's always been. And you know what? He's not going to be. But you just be patient. He'll figure it all out in time.

No one in this town needs to hear the report that plays hourly on KGLD lamenting the end of the brief span of Indian summer weather. And no one is surprised to see a few flakes of snow mixed with the day's cold, slanting rain. No one in this part of the country needs to be told what's on the way or what must end. Nor does anyone need to be told what preparations must be made. The windows on the Witt home still wear their summer screens, and the wind blows hard enough that, on the north side of the house, raindrops are pushed through the screens and streak the glass.

In the dining room all the talk comes from Homer. The business with the hatchet, he says in his high, pinched voice, nodding in the direction of George's swaddled hand, is a new one. But tales about the wild Weboys and their goddamn vicious ways have been going around for years—usually stopping short of murder, but there's some argument on that point. You were at their place—you probably caught on that not all those cars scattered around are registered in the Weboy name. Some of them they probably stole outright, others they bought from someone else who stole them. One of the stories I heard had them cutting the nuts off a Livingston man who cheated them on a car deal. The Weboys can pull any kind of shenanigan they've a mind to, but anyone tries to turn the tables on them, they're squawking and ready to have their revenge. But I've come up with an idea I'd like to run by you.

George listens with the impassive expression of a man who's tried hard to learn the forbearance necessary to be around people who talk too much.

Homer, however, doesn't need permission to continue. He swirls his whiskey, takes a small swallow, then puts the glass down carefully. What do you say we wait until things settle down a bit for you—again he points nonchalantly toward George's injured hand—and then you come back here? We'll round up a few fellows who'd like nothing better than to give the Weboys a taste of their own medicine.

It's obvious that George's fingerless hand bothers him, because he keeps it raised and off to the side as if he can't stand to subject it to anything more than air flowing across the bandage. And what would we do? he asks, his voice as flat as the tabletop.

Do? Hell if I know. Make a raid on the Weboy place. Beat the hell out of those boys. Throw a scare into them once and for all.

These fellows you mention. Tough customers, are they?

They could take care of those Weboys.

And how about the mother?

Maybe we'll take the women along. Homer laughs, a sound like a doll's squeak. I believe their imaginations could come up with a punishment for Blanche.

Like rip her grandchild away from her?

Do what?

George flicks his question away as if it were a crumb. He says, It was the uncle wielded the hatchet. Bill Weboy.

That sonofabitch. We'll come up with something special for him. I tell you, when he showed up here last night I should have got out my twelve-gauge. I could have pulled the trigger on that bastard and spared the world a lot of trouble and grief.

He was *here*? George presses his good hand down on the table as if his question pertained to the very place where he's sitting.

Margaret didn't tell you?

She did not.

Huh. Yeah, he came walking up the street like this was his neighborhood and he was out for his nightly constitutional. Homer raises his watered-down whiskey to his lips and takes another carefully rationed sip. I can't say we put the run on him exactly, he continues, but we sure as hell made it plain he wasn't welcome.

Not like he gives a good goddamn about that.

Say this for the Weboys—they aren't lacking for gall.

Was he alone? asks George.

Oh hell no. He had a carload with him.

Donnie with them?

I couldn't tell. Does it matter? He's with them whether he's with them or not. The Weboys are so damn tight you couldn't fit a shim between them.

Just wondering, says George, if Donnie always has someone else ready to do his dirty work for him.

That mother of his has been cleaning up his messes since he was a kid. Both his and his brothers'.

Margaret and Adeline enter the dining room. Oh please, Margaret says, no more of the Weboys.

Homer laughs his high, strangled laugh. Just like that? Snap your fingers and no more Weboys?

I heard, says George, they paid a visit last night. He looks back and forth from one woman to the other but his look of accusation lingers longest on Adeline.

Can't we not talk about them for the rest of the day? pleads Margaret.

So the talk turns away from the Weboy clan as if that subject could be avoided like a stretch of bad road. Soon it's difficult to imagine that anyone at this table is grieving, defeated, exhausted, or maimed, though one of the group says little, no matter whether the topic is roof shingling (which Homer Witt did back in June), soldiers fighting in Korea (where U.S. fortunes have not fared well recently), or seasons shifting (the Witts saw their last snow in April, the Blackledges in June). No, there's not a reason in the world to believe that anyone sitting at this table is less than whole. Unless Margaret Blackledge reaching over and cutting her husband's food into bite-size chunks is likely to bring such a thought to mind. Or perhaps something out of the ordinary is suggested when the Blackledges stand at the front door and say their thank-yous and good-byes and make their promises to stay in touch, and Adeline reaches out for an actual touch. I still think, she says, and once again the back of her hand approaches George's forehead, you might be running a fever. But he merely leans away from her touch and repeats his two o'clock in the morning lie. I'm fine.

35.

THEY ARE BARELY OUTSIDE GLADSTONE'S CITY LIMITS when George says, You should have told me the uncle showed up last night.

I intended to. The wipers keep the windshield clear but Margaret still grips the steering wheel with both hands and squints out at the highway.

When?

Oh, I don't know. Someday. Soon.

George leans against the passenger door, his injured hand held aloft and his face against the cool window glass. His hat is beside him on the car seat. He says, Not soon enough.

What does it matter?

It's one more Weboy telling us to get the hell out of town.

It's advice I'm happy to take. The snow that earlier mixed with the rain has now changed to ice pellets, and a few of these accumulate on the wiper blades and leave arcing streaks on the glass.

Is that the way he gave it? asks George. As advice? Or an order?

I don't know, George. And I can't see how that matters either.

Almost a mile passes before George answers. It matters.

After another long silence, Margaret says, Ice on the road . . .

None of it's sticking.

. . . makes me think of the night the twins were born. Do you remember?

I remember.

Slow down, I kept telling you. Slow down . . .

I remember.

Margaret allows herself the briefest glance at her husband. His eyes are closed. And why did we decide to drive to the hospital, anyway? Wasn't the plan to call Mrs. Gustafson?

You didn't want to call in the middle of the night. Besides, we thought we had time.

And we did. Even creeping along on the ice, we had time.

Just not as much as we thought we'd have.

Margaret lets up slightly on the accelerator. The car bucks a little as if in protest over the slower speed. The bluffs in the distance have turned a deeper orange-red in the wet weather.

Abruptly George sits straight up. Pull off the road at that turnout up ahead.

What's wrong?

Just pull over.

Are you going to be sick?

Pull over, goddamnit!

Margaret does as she's told. She signals that she intends to turn, slows almost to a stop, and then, with a deliberate hand-over-hand motion, she steers the big car across the highway, bumping off the pavement to a cleared gravel area. This is where they parked when they were on their way *into*

Gladstone, the small scenic lookout from which they first gazed down on a river fringed and furred by cottonwoods, a prairie punctuated with bunchgrass and sagebrush, and a town that was their destination, spread out and sparkling in the distance. The nearby rocky outcrop with its familiar shape of the inverted bowling pin has also taken on a darker tone in the rain, a shade close to bronze.

With his good hand, George reaches across his body and clumsily pulls on the door handle and simultaneously shoves with his shoulder against the door. When it opens, the smell of wet sage and clay rushes into the car.

George almost tumbles out but he stops himself, only to sit bent over and breathing hard on the car's running board.

By now Margaret has climbed out of the car, hurried around, and is squatting in the gray mud in front of her husband. Are you all right? George? Her voice trembles more than usual. Talk to me. Are you all right?

I'm fine, he says, though plainly he is not.

Were you carsick? Was that it? She lowers her head and twists it around so she can look up into her husband's eyes. George?

I'm all right.

Is it your hand that's bothering you?

I needed to stop. That's all.

Won't you tell me—

I'm all right. I told you.

Stiffly she stands up. When she was crouching down, the car door sheltered her from the rain, but now the drops, icy and fine, pelt the sides of her face. She brushes at them as if they were summer gnats swarming and catching in her hair. She looks down at her husband and then takes a step back from him.

Babies. Animals. Men like this one. At some point, if you cannot divine what troubles them, you must step away. You must. Step away and wait.

Here's something else I should have told you, Margaret says, though she's not looking at her husband as she speaks. She gazes in the direction of Gladstone, visible but as if through a veil. When we were at the Witts'? And we were talking about that battle in Korea? I've forgotten the name already, but it sounded like something from a song or a poem. Anyway, I thought, well, if the army comes along to scoop up Jimmy for whatever war's going on when he's old enough to fight, at least I won't have to see him go. Let Lorna see him off, Lorna and his other grandmother. So you see, I'm adjusting. Already. I'm making the best of things.

When she wipes at her face now it's with a gesture that has nothing to do with any swarm of insects. Too late for you, George, but I'm coming around.

With his left hand he grabs the armrest on the car door and with a determined effort manages to push and pull himself to his feet. Now the rain can get at him as well.

Drive there, George says, pointing off to the northwest. I've had enough traveling.

She follows his pointing finger with a look of horror, as if he were suggesting she drive them off the edge of the bluff.

There's a road, he says. You see it? Not the route we took before. Over there. Farther on ahead.

That's not much of a road, George. And why would I drive us there? You've had enough traveling? Well, I've had enough camping. And I mean enough to last me forever.

He folds himself back into the car. Close my door, he says to Margaret. Close it and let's go. He raises his finger-less hand in the air and holds it there in what has become its customary position. He lets his head fall back on the car seat, closes his eyes, and says again, *Go.*

<u>36.</u>

ANOTHER HOUR OF RAIN AND THIS MUDDY, ROCKY
path might wash out completely, but the raindrops now
are so widely spaced the wipers are hardly necessary.
Nevertheless, Margaret must descend with the car in second gear and her foot frequently touching the brake. She
tries to keep the Hudson's wheels in the twin tracks that
snake back and forth down the steep grade. When one tire
slips out of its rut the car rocks precariously, but Margaret
keeps them on course. Is it only the narrow road that holds
her attention? She presses her tongue between her teeth
and her eyes widen with concentration, yet her brow is
unfurrowed as if at this moment she is content to have to
make no decision more important than whether to move
the steering wheel inches to the left or right.

Even when she asks the question, Where are we going,
George? her voice seems animated by no real curiosity or
urgency.

He sits forward and scans the valley floor. There, he says.
Drive there.

Once again, Margaret allows his finger to direct her gaze.

The road, such as it is, gives out at the base of the bluff,
and there, on a flat, bare parcel of land the size of a baseball
diamond, sits a shack, its asphalt shingles as gray as the

sky. Traces of green paint cling to the nearby outhouse, but its boards have weathered to the color of dust. The ground around the shack looks as though it's been picked clean of stones, smoothed, and swept. Next to the door of the shack leans a fishing rod.

Margaret stops fifty feet from the dwelling. Where in hell are we, George?

For answer, he reaches over and presses on the car's horn. Its loud nasal bleat bounces from one rocky wall of the canyon to another and then seems to find its way back inside the car. As soon as the echo fades, George pushes on the horn again, this time holding it down until its wail becomes almost unbearable.

The door of the shack opens and Alton Dragswolf peers out.

All right, says George. Turn off the car. We're here.

No, George. Please. Nevertheless, Margaret does as he commands and turns off the ignition. No, she says again. No. We don't belong here. It is her husband she is pleading with, but she addresses these words to his hat on the seat between them.

Alton Dragswolf has exited the shack completely and he is cautiously walking toward the car. He paws at the air as if this light rain could be pushed aside like a curtain.

George picks up his hat and jams it onto his head, pulling the brim low over his eyes.

George is first out of the car and he raises his injured hand in greeting. Mr. Dragswolf, George calls out.

Alton Dragswolf bends down and squints, as if all the problems of recognition are on his side.

George says again, louder, Mr. Dragswolf!

Margaret gets out of the car, and when she does, Alton Dragswolf's look of bewilderment vanishes and his customary smile returns. Come for a visit, did you? he says cheerily. Damned if I can remember your name.

The Blackledges, George says, striding forward. George and Margaret.

Alton Dragswolf nods enthusiastically as if to express his pleasure at George's correct answer. That's right, that's right!

This is your place?

Free and clear. You found it, all right.

And is your invitation still good?

Although no vehicle is visible on the grounds, Alton Dragswolf's grease-streaked coveralls give him the look of someone who's been working under the hood of his car. He pulls a stained bandanna out of his pocket and wipes his hands. If he remembers his invitation, the recollection doesn't show in his eyes.

You said we were welcome to put up here, George reminds him. I'd like to take you up on that, if you're willing. We have some miles ahead of us, but once we got on the road, damned if I didn't find that I'm not up to the journey. Not just yet, anyway.

Margaret has taken her place at her husband's side. She pinches the fabric of his shirtsleeve as if she needs to stay close but without letting him know that she's hanging on tight.

We can pay, George continues. Cash or goods. Or both.

She looks up at him as if this speech of his could not have been stranger had he opened his mouth and let loose with a coyote's howl.

Don't you know nothing about Indians? Alton Dragswolf says. We're famous for our hospitality. And for giving away what white people charge big money for.

Crow? George asks. Or Blackfoot?

Nope. Black*feet*. I got two. Alton kicks up first one foot and then the other. Thanks for asking, though.

He hurries around behind the Blackledges, his scurrying steps raising dust even upon the rain-dampened earth. He makes shooing gestures toward them. Let's go, let's go. Inside. I don't want my guests standing out here getting older and colder!

For all the force and volume of George's speech of a moment ago, he now walks with halting, short strides toward the shack. Margaret is careful to remain close at his side, the exact distance a parent keeps when a child takes his first steps. Alton Dragswolf rushes ahead and opens the door for them.

And then George and Margaret Blackledge, who have spent so few of their nights under a roof not their own, once again enter a stranger's house.

The home of Alton Dragswolf is one wide room divided into three areas according to their function. They have entered at the middle, into a kitchen. A bedroom is at one end, a work and storage room at the other, and although the interior is full of boxes, cans, and jars of foodstuffs, all of it is neatly stacked and carefully arranged on shelves and cupboards. Next to the cookstove is a woodbox filled with small logs, even in length and circumference. Above a worktable at the far end of the room, tools hang from hooks on a pegboard. At the near end is a made bed. There are no dirty dishes, silverware, or cookware in the galvanized steel sink, just a dripping pump looming over the sink's depths. A dishrag hangs over the pump's handle. The floors are bare and look recently swept. The shack's interior smells of the food old people eat, the cabbage, carrots, rutabagas, and other roots that they boil into soups that can be eaten for days.

Can I get you something to eat? Alton asks.

It's kind of you to offer, says Margaret, but we had a big lunch not long ago.

Should I put on the coffee?

Margaret glances at her husband.

Not for me, says George. He looks as though he needs to sit down, and not many choices are available—three mismatched wooden chairs pushed up against the kitchen table and, over by the bed, a high-backed rocking chair.

In spite of George's worn-out, weary appearance, Alton Dragswolf reaches up to a shelf and brings down a deck of cards. Either of you play gin rummy?

If it's all right with you, Mr. Dragswolf, I think my husband would like to lie down.

Oh, sure, sure. It's not entertainment you need. It's rest. Sure. He says this as though he's recalling a book lesson. Sorry. Where are my manners?

Margaret says, Your manners, Mr. Dragswolf, are perfect. We're the ones who should be apologizing. Barging in on you unannounced like this.

With his hopping little steps, the young man leads his guests toward one end of the shack. The day is overcast and Alton Dragswolf has lit none of his lamps, so the bedroom area is almost as dark as night, its single, small window covered by a towel hanging over a curtain rod.

Alton Dragswolf turns back a corner of the dark wool blanket covering the bed. When he does, he exposes sheets so white they gleam in the dim light. He tries to fluff the pillow, but it's so flattened by years of heavy-headed sleepers that the action is futile. Alton pats the sagging mattress. Here you go.

George sits on the edge of the bed. My boots, he says.

Margaret turns her back to her husband, bends over, and pulls his booted foot up between her legs. She pulls one boot off with her own strength and then as she reaches for the other foot she slaps her own ass and says, Go ahead. Push.

Reluctantly George puts his stocking foot on his wife's backside and Margaret removes the other boot. She laughs as though they had been performing this routine for the delight of an audience. George collapses on the mattress, its springs squealing as if receiving weight for the first time. His eyes close immediately, and he carefully lays his injured hand across his chest.

Margaret and Alton Dragswolf stand over the bed, both of them looking solemnly down on George Blackledge.

Can you die from getting your fingers chopped off? asks Alton.

Jesus Christ, says George. I'm not deaf. His eyes remain closed.

Well? Can you?

No, Margaret says, gently laying a hand on Alton's shoulder. You can't.

George's eyes open and he says, But it plays hell with getting your boots off and on.

I was just wondering, says Alton. Because I heard all about what the Weboys done to you. Except I didn't know it was you.

George props himself up on his elbows. What did you hear? His eyes are open now.

That you got your fingers chopped off. What else?

Who told you?

I got an uncle lives in Gladstone but he drives out here every couple days to see if I need anything. He was in Antler's—that's pretty much a cowboy bar, but it don't bother him to go in there—and he heard you pulled a gun on the Weboy brothers and then got your fingers chopped off for your trouble.

Who'd your uncle hear this from?

Hell, everybody was talking about it. I told you about the Weboys before, didn't I? How they're sort of famous around here. Famous for being sonsabitches. What my uncle didn't say but I was wondering about—was it like a quick draw or something? You went for your gun and he beat you to the draw with a tomahawk?

George lowers himself back down to the pillow. Not exactly.

My husband, says Margaret, her voice vibrating with indignation, was defending me.

Yeah? Against all them Weboys? I don't know how smart that was. But you'd sure as hell need a gun for that job. A gun and then some.

Margaret puts her finger to her lips. Maybe he'll nap if we get out of here, she says, backing away from the bed.

Go fishing, you mean? says Alton. Because that's what I was going to do once the rain let up.

By all means. Don't let us upset your plans.

Plans? Alton Dragswolf laughs. I don't have plans. I just go fishing when I want to go fishing.

At this Margaret smiles. Then you should go fishing.

You want to come? I got another rod somewheres.

You go ahead. I'll stay here and keep my husband company.

Well, don't do nothing for supper. In case I catch something.

I'll make a deal with you, Mr. Dragswolf. Any fish you catch I'll clean and fry up for us.

He grabs his tackle box from beside the door and hurries out like a boy dismissed from school.

37.

In Alton Dragswolf's absence, Margaret wanders back and forth from one end of the shack to the other, returning every few minutes to the bedside to check on her husband, who seems, after much stretching, folding, and rearranging of his body and its limbs, to have fallen asleep. His customary sleeping position, with his right hand curled at his head like a dog or cat's paw, isn't available to him. Every time he brings his bandaged hand near his face, he winces as though he can't bear the smell of himself.

On Alton Dragswolf's workbench Margaret finds tufts of fur and feathers, shining strips of metal, and hooks of various sizes. The young man makes his own fishing lures. And he marks time. Framed between claw and ball peen hammers on the pegboard is a Northern Pacific calendar, the days crossed out with precise *X*s and the ever-passing present thus consigned to the past. I'll be damned, Margaret says softly. It's October. The photograph for the month features a flock of geese arrowing their way across a morning sky, clear but for a few feathery, orange-tinted clouds. Or is that an evening sky?

Near the workbench is the shack's only evidence of Alton Dragswolf's Indian heritage. Hanging from a nail is a beautiful buckskin outfit, shirt and leggings, beaded, beribboned, fringed, and its leather tanned and treated so it's as soft as flannel. The garments could as easily be hanging in a museum. There's no evidence that Alton Dragswolf has any use for them but this display.

In the kitchen Margaret inspects a large cast-iron skillet sitting on the cookstove. If she prepares supper tonight, she'll use this pan and build a fire under it, exactly how she learned to cook in her mother's kitchen. She wipes a finger across the surface of the skillet. Alton Dragswolf keeps his cookware as clean as everything else in his home.

The next time her circuit takes her to the far end of the shack, she finds George lying on his back with his eyes open.

How are you doing? she asks. Did that nap help?

Is the boy here?

I expect he'll stay away as long as he can. That way he won't have to worry about entertaining us.

George pushes himself up to a sitting position. She watches the process carefully. You know, she says, I was thinking earlier about all the smiling folks we've met since we crossed over into the state. And how you can't trust a one of them. The sober-sided ones, on the other hand, like your friend Nevelsen, seem a pretty steady bunch. Adeline, certainly. That young doctor whose name I can never remember—

Wyatt.

That's right. Wyatt. But then we arrive here and young Mr. Dragswolf can't seem to wipe that grin off his face. And I'd count him among the trustworthy ones, wouldn't you?

Unless he's out there right now plotting a way to do us in.

George pats his shirt pocket for his cigarettes.

I put them up here, says Margaret and takes the pack of Lucky Strikes from the top of Alton Dragswolf's three-drawer dresser. When I look around this place, she says, though her eyes are fixed on the cigarette pack, and I see the life Mr. Dragswolf has made for himself, I can imagine James doing something like this. Living by himself on his own corner of the homestead, running a small string of horses—

Don't. He barks out that command like he's training an animal. But then his voice lowers. The boy's dead and buried. Do yourself some good and leave off that line of thinking.

Is that what you do, George? You don't allow yourself to even think about your son?

That'd make about as much sense as poking at the holes where my fingers used to be.

You think love's like a wound, George? You let it scab over, then forget about it?

I don't believe in seeing our son where he can't be. And I don't see anything of him in Alton Dragswolf. Who strikes me as more than a little strange.

Oh, he means well. Finally she puts the cigarette between George's lips and strikes a match for him. She looks around the shack, and when she sees a battered tin ashtray on the kitchen table she retrieves it and places it alongside her husband. He's probably just lost track of things a bit, living out here. As near as I can tell, there isn't a clock in the place.

Another one of your theories? George says. Could be.

We could drive off, you know. I could write him a note and tell him we headed for home. Maybe leave him a few dollars for his trouble. And we could be back in Dalton in a few hours.

I'm not ready.

You're not ready? What does that mean? You're not ready . . .

I'm not ready to go home.

Oh, George. She presses her hands to her face. Please. You never wanted to leave in the first place. How can you not be ready to go back? When she brings her hands down, her eyes are glittering with unspilled tears. Please.

For an answer he turns his head away and blows a stream of smoke toward the towel-covered window.

Margaret Blackledge takes the cigarette from her husband. She crushes it out and puts the ashtray on top of the dresser. Move over, you old bag of bones. She climbs into the bed and presses the length of her body along George's. She rests her chin on his chest and when she does, the tremor stops, though perhaps some of her trembling enters him. She slips her hand inside his shirt, popping open one of the snaps in the process. Do you want to go the other way? she asks. We could do that. The car is still packed with supplies. We could head west . . . just drive and see where we land. See an ocean, maybe. Or we could go north . . . see if your friend will let us bunk down in his jail again.

I told you. I'm done traveling.

You're done traveling. What does that *mean*, George? Look where we are. We can't stay here. We don't *belong* here. Her hand moves around on his chest as if she's probing for a heartbeat.

George keeps staring off in the direction of the window. The October sun sets early and today it hasn't even made an appearance. On the other side of the towel and the glass, the day is all but done.

George? You're not planning to die on me, are you?

With that hand inside his shirt she grabs a tuft of his chest hair and pulls hard. He flinches. *Are you, George?*

He turns slowly toward her and with the hand that has all its fingers he lifts her head tenderly toward his own. A man doesn't die from losing a few fingers, he says. I heard you say so myself.

38.

Alton Dragswolf did not catch any fish, but Margaret prepares supper anyway. She has brought groceries from the car—Spam, potatoes for frying, a can of creamed corn, a jar of applesauce—because, she insisted, it wouldn't be right for them to eat Alton's food.

While she works at the cookstove, Alton and George sit at the kitchen table, George sipping whiskey from a coffee cup and smoking. Since he has found a way to strike matches with one hand, he no longer asks his wife to light his cigarettes for him. He pins the matchbook to the table, folds a match in half, and rasps it into flame with his thumb. Alton, who neither drinks nor smokes, deals poker hands to himself from a limp, dog-eared deck of cards.

As Margaret sets the table, she says to Alton, I hope you don't mind, but I was admiring your fancy buckskins in there.

I don't mind. But they ain't mine. They're my uncle's. He don't miss many powwows.

They're simply beautiful.

Alton says, He keeps them here so's his wife don't take it and sell them. Myself, I ain't much for dancing.

Two kerosene lamps keep at bay the darkness gathered

at each end of the shack. The bracket lamp on the wall next to the door has a bulbous chimney and casts a wide, diffuse glow. The lamp on the table has a narrow chimney and its light is so intense it seems as if its purpose were to reveal the character of any man or woman sitting nearby. Its flame is not bright enough, however, to keep the deep-cut features of George Blackledge's face from looking like shadows.

Margaret brings the skillet to the table but George puts his hand over his plate. Not for me, he says.

You need to eat something, she says.

Maybe a little applesauce.

That's not enough for you, she says, but she moves on to Alton.

Put it all on here, says Alton. I'm hungry enough to eat the asshole out of a dead skunk.

She heaps his plate with fried potatoes and thick slabs of Spam. I'll pass on the corn, he says. Me and vegetables don't agree.

Alton pours ketchup onto his meat and potatoes and then shakes salt and pepper liberally over both.

Margaret Blackledge spoons applesauce into a bowl and sets it before her husband, but he pushes it away. She sits demurely at George's side. In spite of insisting that George eat, she has put nothing on her own plate.

You mentioned your uncle, Margaret says. Do you have other family around here?

His mouth full, Alton merely shakes his head.

This isn't the land of your ancestors? Margaret smiles politely.

Nah. Just mine. The land and the house both.

Northern Montana's Blackfoot country, isn't it? asks George.

I guess. But I ain't Blackfeet.

I thought—

I was making a joke. You know, like I had two feet. And they was both black. But I thought you knew. I like fishing too much to be a Blackfeet. They ain't much for fishing, you know. Too damn superstitious or something. Nah, I'm Arikara and Hidatsa. My folks were, anyway. From North Dakota. But they're both dead.

Oh, Alton, I'm sorry, Margaret says. Then she adds brightly, We're from North Dakota. She moves the bowl of applesauce back in front of George.

Yeah, I seen your license plates that first day. Are there any more potatoes?

Margaret rises and goes back to the stove. So, Margaret says, this isn't where you're from, Alton?

Alton Dragswolf shrugs. It's just where I am.

She scrapes the remaining potatoes onto his plate and Alton proceeds to cover them once again with ketchup, salt, and pepper.

There's nothing wrong with your appetite, Mr. Dragswolf.

He moves the potatoes to his mouth with a spoon. Between mouthfuls, Alton says, My aunt used to call me Bug because I like potatoes so much. You know, like potato bug. That was before she got so damn mean she wouldn't call me anything.

I'm sorry to hear that.

Doesn't bother me. I don't have to live with her.

Or anyone else, says George.

Or anyone else. You bet. He pushes himself back from the table. I like the way you fix potatoes, he says to Margaret.

Instead of slicing them, I usually cut them up in little squares and pyramids and then if I have an onion I chop it up and fry it in there too. But this way is good. Hey, do you want dessert? Look in that drawer there.

Margaret opens a drawer near the sink and finds it full of packages of Switzer's licorice. Mr. Dragswolf, you have a sweet tooth.

Yeah, and before long it'll probably be my only one, the way the others are rotting away. Alton clacks his teeth together. That's the only bad thing about living out here—what if I run out of licorice?

Neither George nor Margaret want any of the candy but Alton tears open the cellophane package eagerly and soon has its entire contents in his mouth. Sort of like chewing tobacco, he says, his tongue working clumsily around the black wad. Especially if I spit.

Not indoors, Alton.

Margaret pumps enough water into a large pot to do the dishes and still have plenty for all of them to wash up for the evening. She lifts the kettle onto the back boiler burner and feeds another log into the woodbox. While she works, the men sit silently at the table, Alton with his licorice and his playing cards, George with his cigarettes and his whiskey.

Finally George Blackledge says to Alton, Do you work?

Not like you mean, answers Alton. But *you* try rounding up enough wood around these parts to get through a winter. Or try casting a line all day into water where there ain't no fish. You'll find out what real work is. Besides, he says and tears off another strip of licorice, I have to be available in case I get houseguests.

Behind them Margaret laughs. Touché!

What do you do for money? asks George.

I got some insurance when my folks died. That's how I bought this place.

So you're a man of independent means.

I get by. And I don't hurt nobody doing it. How about you? What do you do to earn a dollar?

George inhales deeply but it's only oxygen that puffs up his chest. I hold up boards for another man to hammer.

Hey, that's work I could maybe handle! Alton crawls his fingers across the table until they're almost touching George's bandaged hand. Can you do it, Alton asks, without fingers?

I don't know. I'll have to find out.

I'd use it for an excuse. Sorry! I can't hold up no more boards! Get yourself another man!

They probably will get another man. If they haven't already.

Margaret throws the dish towel over her shoulder and approaches the table. She puts her arms around her husband's neck. Mr. Blackledge, she informs Alton, was once a sheriff.

Alton Dragswolf leans back in his chair as though he needs to get a better look at George. No shit? He turns his thumbs and index fingers into blazing six-shooters. *Blam, blam, blam!* So were you fast on the draw? A dead-eye shot?

George stubs out his cigarette. I couldn't hit the broad side of a barn.

Did you ever shoot anybody?

Nope.

Well, did you ever shoot and miss?

No. I never pointed a gun at anyone. George picks up his

pack of cigarettes, then puts it down again with a sigh. Striking a match is still a complicated business. Most sheriffs, George says, do a hell of a lot more typing than shooting.

Is that what you'd say when you were running for office? I'm the best damn typer in the county?

Not the best . . .

Of course, no more typing for you, says Alton as, with all ten fingers, he mimics tapping away at a keyboard.

No, not for me.

Too bad. Because that beats hell out of holding up a board for another man to pound, don't it?

By this much, George says and holds up his bandaged hand. He wears a look of momentary satisfaction, as if he's finally found the use to which he can put that span of air between thumb and little finger.

. . .

Alton insists that the Blackledges take his bed for the night, and in turn Margaret helps him make up a pallet on the floor on the other end of the shack.

When Margaret wishes him good night, she tells him again how grateful they are for his hospitality.

I invited you, Alton says shyly. You came. Stay as long as you like.

Perhaps it is not only the sincerity in Alton Dragswolf's voice but also a light in his eyes that says he too is grateful that makes Margaret do what she does. She puts her arms around him and kisses him on the cheek. You know what I wish, Alton? I wish my grandson would grow up to be like you.

Yeah? Well, I bet he won't—wish that, I mean.

. . .

Later, when Margaret lies in bed with her leg thrown across her husband and she can hear from his breathing that he's still awake, she whispers, I have an idea, George.

A long moment passes before he says, Let's hear it.

Now, let me finish before you make fun of me. And if you don't know what to say, don't say anything—not that you'll have a problem in that regard. Sleep on it, if need be.

Let's hear it.

Why don't we move here? And I don't mean to Gladstone. I mean right *here*. In with Alton. He'd be glad of the company, I bet. And the help. I could do the cooking. You'd help him expand the place. We could put another room on the backside of the kitchen—

Let me guess: I'd hold up the boards and he'd drive the nails.

Stop it, George. We'd be close enough to Gladstone that I could see Mrs. Witt from time to time. I swear, after only a few days she's become more of a friend to me than any woman I've ever known. And Jimmy—

I should have known. Jimmy.

You said you'd let me finish.

You're finished now. Jesus Christ, woman. When will you stop torturing yourself? So we move in here with this Indian kid and we buy him his licorice or whatever the hell your plan is. Then what? You drive into town every day and park outside Jimmy's school? Hang out by the playground and try to catch a glimpse of him? Stand across the street from Montgomery Ward and see if he comes with his uncle or his stepfather to pick up Lorna? My God, Margaret!

Keep your voice down. You'll wake Alton.

Maybe we should wake him. George's anger has not cooled by a degree but his voice softens. Let him hear what a crazy goddamn idea is churning through that brain of yours. Maybe even a chucklehead like Alton Dragswolf can make you see things clear.

All right, George.

A few hours ago you were ready to head off to California if that was what I wanted. Now you want to leave behind all the life you've ever known to live in a little shack in a valley without so much as a real road leading in or out.

I said, all right.

If husbands and wives know anything, it is when the pursuit of argument is futile. They might go on, but they know.

Margaret Blackledge turns away from her husband. She lies on the side of the bed closest to the wall and she reaches out now and places her palm against the rough wood as if she feared its encroachment. After James died she could keep her eyes dry throughout the day by filling every hour with one chore after another. But if all that work failed to exhaust her, the night would be another matter. As she and George lay in bed together, if so much as a single sob got away from her, he would rise, even if he'd been sound asleep, and go sit in his rocking chair in the parlor. Was it a calculation on his part? Before long her mother-grief would diminish, if only by a degree, replaced by the wife-worry of when her husband would return to her side. When the mattress sagged again under his weight, they would both sleep at last.

39.

WHEN MARGARET WAKES, THE DARKNESS IN THE shack is so complete it seems to have substance, as if night had wrapped every sleeper in a caul. She reaches out her hand and touches empty space where George's body had been.

Go back to sleep. The voice comes from above her and then her eyes penetrate this membrane of gloom. It's George and he's standing beside the bed. He has pulled on his jeans and his shirt but his belt is not buckled and the shirt not snapped. I'm going out to the privy.

Margaret starts to get out of bed.

Lie down, he commands her. When I need someone to wipe my ass I'll let you know. I think I can manage to take a piss on my own. Jesus.

Before she climbed into bed for the night, Margaret took a last look outside. Fog no higher than a man's waist clung like smoke to the valley floor. Now when George opens the door she feels the cooler air and in her fatigue it seems as if the fog itself were entering and winding its way back to her and then as though the fog were indistinguishable from the haze that sleep brings.

· · ·

Who can say what wakes a wife and tells her that the space beside her has been vacant for too long? The feel of absence? The sounds that don't fit the hour?

The whine of a car's engine, as it has a hill to climb and fog to struggle through.

The whir of a partridge, its nest in the brush disturbed by a car's headlights.

The sheet where he lay is cool. And damp, as if with fever sweat.

The spark that flies between the synapses of the long-married travels too far and fires too hard and in effect says, He's gone.

Margaret rushes to the door and throws it open in time to see the Hudson climbing the road and almost to the top of the bluff, free of the low-lying fog, its taillights tingeing pink the dust that billows behind the car.

Oh God, oh my God. Oh George. These words she barely whispers. These she shouts: George! George! Stop!

Then Alton Dragswolf wakes. Something's not right. A door open? A woman calling out? He crawls out of his blankets, pushes himself to his feet, and makes his way to the open door.

He arrives in time to see Margaret Blackledge running from his shack and futilely chasing a car that labors up the hill, bouncing and tilting over the rocks and ruts, its engine whining with effort.

Margaret's nightgown reaches well below her knees and the flannel binds her strides and she reaches down and lifts the hem almost to her waist so she can run, run, run after the Hudson. She's barefoot and she slips in the mud and stones cut and bruise her feet and when her path begins to ascend the hill the tough, wiry brush scratches and cuts her bare legs and burs and low branches catch at the flannel and she calls one more time, George! Stop!

And is it juniper brush too that scrapes the finish of the Hudson, or is it an outcropping of rock as George drives too close to the bluff's wall? No matter. George has never been like some of the men living in this part of the world, who care more for their machinery than their animals, and he keeps the Hudson on its narrow climbing course.

Then the car crests the hill, its headlights sending twin beams into the sky like searchlights. The taillights wink. The engine's complaint drops an octave and begins to hum a smoother song. The Hudson and her husband vanish from Margaret's sight.

She drops the hem of her nightgown, and by the time she reaches the valley floor, the bottom half of the garment is wet with the rain she's swept from the tall grass.

Alton meets her at the base of the hill. Hey, he says.

He's gone, Alton.

Yeah, I can see.

What can we *do*, Alton? How can we stop him and bring him back?

Maybe he'll just come back. All on his own. Alton Dragswolf hops up and down. Hey, my feet are freezing. I got to go in.

Margaret is slower to give up, but finally the hopelessness of staring at night and fog overcomes her and she returns to the shack.

Alton has lit the lamp on the table and its light discloses Margaret's condition—her wet nightgown, her scratched and mud-streaked legs. Her feet dark not only with dirt but with blood.

Jesus, missus!

What? Oh. She appraises herself. I'm all right. Look how I'm tracking up your floor, she says but doesn't move.

I'll fill up my washtub for you, Alton says but he remains in place as well. Where do you suppose he's going? Probably to town, huh?

The way a woman would respond to her child's cry, Margaret suddenly hurries to the part of the shack that had served as their bedroom. She opens George's suitcase and drops to the floor in order to feel frantically around its interior. When she finds the bottle of whiskey she stops searching, rises stiffly, and walks slowly, helplessly, back out to the kitchen area.

There she finds Alton Dragswolf with a boot in each hand and a puzzled expression on his face. He took my tackle box, Alton says. He left his boots and took my tackle box.

. . .

The Hudson's interior smells hot, of overheated grease or oil or a burning hose or belt or of machine parts gnashing against each other, the result no doubt of George taxing the car not only by making it climb out of the valley in first gear but by remaining in that gear as the trail began to level off. But that was only because he couldn't work the gearshift, not at first, not with his bandaged hand.

Now, however, he's learned to manage. Gripping the shift lever is impossible, yet he can maneuver it into second gear with the heel of his hand and pull it down into third by making a sort of claw of his palm and two fingers.

After that rough ascent out of the valley, the highway, smooth and straight as unspooling ribbon, is a relief. The fog has lifted too, adding to the sense of easy rolling. When the road drops down from the second ridge and Gladstone comes into view, its lights are clustered under low clouds whose bottoms have a faint lavender glow. It's a sight as inviting as a featherbed to a tired man.

But Gladstone is not George Blackledge's destination. It's where he'll start, since only from there can he find the way.

The city is mostly shut down for the night, though much of its neon still blinks and flickers and glows for businesses that won't unlock their doors again for hours. Here and there a bar is open and maybe in one of them there's a bartender who wouldn't ask a man where his boots or his fingers are . . .

But George keeps the Hudson moving, and carefully within the speed limits. Who knows—the sheriff or a deputy might be waiting in that alley between Woolworth's and the Red Trail Meat Market or behind the statue of the Hereford on the Keogh County Fairgrounds, waiting for someone who doesn't think the traffic laws apply in the middle of the night. In his lawman days George would let such drivers pass unless they seemed on their way to or from misconduct. And what made him believe he could know such a thing? Perhaps from the frightened, desperate, or determined look of the man behind the wheel.

. . .

The last mile George drives with his lights off, the Hudson slowed to a pace little more than a man's brisk walk. He's traveling by feel and memory now. The roadbed is unevenly distributed gravel, and when those stones no longer crunch under the tires or ping against the muffler, it means he has strayed into the soft dirt between the road and the ditch.

But then he sees enough, just enough. The fence-line. The broken gate hanging open. He eases the car into the ditch and shuts off the engine.

When he climbs out of the car, stubble and stones stab and dig into his stocking feet, but he keeps moving forward. To a man who has set aside his own scruples, a few weeds and rocks present no real obstacle.

Not a light burns in the Weboy house, but its looming shape is enough to steer by. Once George is in the yard, he pauses to be sure of his bearings. Of the cars parked haphazardly between the barn and the house, one is a blue Ford, and at the sight of it, George feels a small shiver of solace. Though the night sky is lightless, the house's windows glint faintly. He counts windows until he can be sure—yes, in that frame stood the woman and her child.

George's way is clear now, and he walks to the door. When he tries the knob, it turns easily. Strange, that thieves do not think to lock their doors . . .

40.

DONNIE WEBOY WAKES GASPING, STARVING FOR AIR, but when he tries to inhale, it feels as though he were breathing in cobwebs, cloth, dust, blood . . . Then he sees. Then he understands. The gun barrel presses hard against his temple.

Don't make a sound, George Blackledge whispers. His bandaged hand—what's left of it—is pressing down on Donnie's nose and mouth. Or I'll put a bullet in your brain. To make his point he cocks the revolver, and in the sleeping house that hammer click makes a sound like a small bone cracking.

Donnie tries to shake his head. Whether it's to free his nose and mouth or to indicate his willingness to comply with George Blackledge's command isn't clear. But he makes no attempt to bring his hands out from the blankets, and though his eyes widen with fear and comprehension, he keeps still. George takes his hand away from Donnie's face but keeps the revolver at his head. Donnie takes a deep silent breath.

It's difficult to believe that the woman at Donnie's side could sleep through this disturbance, but George has to reach across and shake her shoulder and say softly, Lorna. Wake up, Lorna.

Her slumber has been deep but because she's a mother, when Lorna wakes she looks in the wrong direction, toward the corner of the bedroom where her son sleeps on his makeshift bed, a twin-size mattress on the floor.

Then she twists around and, like Margaret Blackledge only an hour earlier, Lorna sees George Blackledge standing over her bed.

Ssh. George takes the gun away from Donnie's head and holds it up for her to see and to understand the situation and its gravity. Quiet, he says. Although the revolver's nickel plating is chipped and worn away, it has enough shine left to glint in the dark room. He swings the gun back down so it can resume its long-barreled gaze at Donnie Weboy's head.

George Blackledge leans closer to Lorna. Do you want to go back to Dalton? he asks. You and the boy? He doesn't say the child's name.

Lorna looks again to her sleeping son.

You have to decide, George says. Go or stay. It is exactly the choice, down to the very wording, that his wife presented to him not a week ago.

How long can a household's slumber be expected to hold with a stranger in its midst? Won't someone soon sense a breath that does not belong? The tread of a foot too heavy, too light, on a creaking board? Won't a dream veer off its course and into danger?

Right now, Lorna.

Lorna, says Donnie.

George jabs the pistol to within an inch of Donnie's eye, and he flinches and his shoulder twists upward as if it wanted to take the bullet.

Not you, George says to Donnie. You don't say a god-damn word. This is up to her. She decides on her own.

Lorna is sitting up now and she's looking not only to where her son sleeps but into every one of the room's dark corners. I don't know . . .

You know what the life will be, George says to her. Here or there, you know. This isn't something you need to think on.

I'll go. *I'll go.* But when she says this she's staring at the gun and perhaps she's only making the choice that will allow her to side with the man who has the weapon.

George lowers the hammer on the revolver. Then pick up the boy and go, he says, permitting himself a quick glance toward the bedroom door. You know our car. It's parked in the ditch at the bottom of the drive. The keys are in it. Get in and drive straight to Gladstone. Go to the hospital and ask for a nurse. Adeline Witt.

To the *hospital*?

That's right. Adeline Witt. A nurse. At the hospital. That's who you ask for. Mrs. Witt.

My things . . . Jimmy's . . . I have to—

No. George shakes his head emphatically. You get out now. You don't take a goddamn thing. You *go.* As quiet as you can out of the house and then once you're out, you run like hell to the car. And Lorna—the front door. You go out the front door.

It's not clear whether understanding or alarm moves Lorna, but now she climbs quickly out of bed. She goes to Jimmy's bed and crouches next to her son. Without making any attempt to wake him first, she lifts him, and her fear and her mother's strength allow her to rise up again with the boy clinging to her.

For the first five or six years of their lives, children are accustomed to sleeping in motion, rolled in carriages or rocked in cradles, patted or swayed in a parent's embrace, carried off to crib or bed, their dreams as continuous as time itself. Jimmy's eyes open but there's no reason to believe that he sees this scene as it is. The faces, after all, are familiar. Here's his mother, his grandfather . . . There's Donnie . . .

And it's Donnie who first speaks the boy's name. Jimmy, he says out loud, half in greeting and half in appeal.

The word is no sooner spoken than George Blackledge jams his fingerless hand against Donnie's mouth and brings the barrel of the revolver down on his skull. The *thock* is like a rock thrown against a hollow tree.

Not from you, whispers George. And strikes Donnie again. The sound of the second blow is muffled because the barrel skids off Donnie's forehead and tears loose a flap of his scalp. Blood flows onto the pillowcase and in the dark room the blood is as black as shoe polish.

Donnie's eyes remain open but he has lost his ability to recognize the moment he's in. His lips make a breathy popping sound as if he's trying to pronounce a word that begins with *b* or *p* but no syllable follows those soft plosives.

Jimmy has seen his grandfather's attack. He sees the blood. But he's four years old. He's only a moment removed from dreaming. There's no reason to think that he'll remember this act. Not without a photograph or someone reminding him over the years of what he once witnessed on an October night.

The sudden violence hurries Lorna on her way but George stops her before she's out the door.

Put on a pair of shoes, he says. The driveway is rocky.

And remember—the front door. George's socks are dark with muck and perhaps blood. Though they are miles apart, husband and wife share an affliction, unbeknownst to the other.

Lorna opens the closet door and steps into a pair of high heels, which she no doubt wore during her day's long shift. But the discomfort of a pair of shoes is nothing compared to George Blackledge's frightful, cold fury, and she totters out of the bedroom and toward the stairs. In addition to her high heels, she's wearing pajamas, the first sold for women in Gladstone's Montgomery Ward.

Donnie has identified the warm wet flow of his own blood and is trying to press the pillow against his wound. This clumsy effort gives him the appearance of a man attempting to suffocate himself. George does nothing to help him but neither does he stop Donnie's moans.

George leaves the bedroom, his footsteps a whispering shuffle on the wood floor, unlike the rapid *clock-clock-clock* of Lorna's steps.

41.

By the time Lorna, carrying Jimmy, has run, slid, and stumbled to the bottom of the long, sloping driveway, flames have filled the back entry of the Weboy house. So fast! But of course that is where all the fuel for a fire—newspapers and magazines, stray pieces of wood, piles of rags—was stored, as well as the kerosene to speed any flames on their way. She stops for a moment to watch—both the blazing house and its billowing smoke stand out against the night sky—and it's at that very instant that the fire bursts through the roof of the back porch and flickers up toward the second floor. The sight brings a gasp from Lorna, though she's already breathless with fright and exertion. Anyone trying to escape the burning house will have to go out the front door, the exit she and Jimmy used, but now it looks as if fire is flickering there as well.

And why *has* no one exited the house? By now someone has surely smelled the smoke, if not felt the heat. And where's Mr. Blackledge? Why would he remain inside a burning house? Shouldn't he be coming down the hill toward her? Unless . . . is that him? It looks as though someone is outside the front door, but whoever it is, he's not moving, though surely he can see the flames from where he stands.

Then, just as Lorna is squinting through the darkness, trying to determine whose form that might be in the wavering shadows cast by the firelight, an explosion of sound—like a door banging, banging, banging . . . And now windows are bursting—shattering as if the panes were being dropped on rocks from a great height; the house's boards and timbers are cracking, and its nails are popping. And in the back entry where the fire burned first and hottest there were boxes of ammunition . . . The acrid smell of smoke is everywhere . . . She can feel it in her nostrils, her lungs . . . She can *taste* it . . .

Lorna doesn't wait any longer. George Blackledge's command is still echoing in her ears and she practically throws her son into the car and then climbs in after him. He's crying now, wide awake, cold, and frightened. His mother pulls him close to her but she makes sure he remains lying down on the car seat.

Lorna turns the key in the ignition. The Hudson's engine is still warm and turns over immediately. Hot air blows from the heater. As she puts the car into gear and begins to drive away, the weeds in the ditch scratch against the undercarriage and then the gravel from the road clatters against the muffler. In the rearview mirror, the burning house colors the sky like a sunset.

. . .

Despite her tears and the Hudson's balky, unfamiliar transmission, despite having to drive sometimes with only one hand on the wheel because she has to pat Jimmy with the other, trying to calm him, trying to make him believe with touch what she cannot convince him of with her sobbed

words—Ssh, there, there, it's going to be all right, it's going
to be fine—despite having to watch the rearview mirror
without even being sure what or whom she's watching for,
despite the darkness and the fog that comes and goes, despite all that, Lorna manages to do as George ordered, to
maneuver those narrow, unmarked county roads and find
the way to Gladstone and then to Good Samaritan Hospital.
She travels that distance under those difficult circumstances
only to find that once she pulls the Hudson crookedly into
the bay usually reserved for the ambulance, she is unable to
open the door and climb out of the car. It's not the lock or
the door handle that are preventing her but something inside her, not terror and not panic but perhaps their sudden
absence and the relief that takes their place, that paralyzes
her, and she can't do anything but press her face against the
window glass and whimper softly, Help, help us.

Carl Skeller, a fair-haired young man no bigger than
a jockey, is the orderly on duty, and when he sees the car
parked dangerously close to the hospital doors, he draws
near to investigate. Then he notices that there's a woman
in the car and runs out to see what this emergency might
be. He opens the door for Lorna and she tumbles out of
the car. She starts immediately for the hospital's bright,
warm interior but then turns back for her son, grabbing
his arm and pulling him from the car as if it were on fire.

Nurse Witt, Lorna says to the orderly. I need to see
Nurse Witt!

And though Carl Skeller should no doubt stay with
this wild-eyed woman and the little boy—after all, one or
both of them must be injured or ill, or else why would she
show up at the hospital in the middle of the night in high

heels and pajamas?—something in the urgency of her de-
mand makes him obey and he hurries off.

Almost ten minutes pass before Carl Skeller finds
Adeline at the second-floor nurses' station drinking coffee
and smoking a cigarette and visiting with a doctor who's been
called to the hospital on a false alarm. Carl tells Mrs. Witt
that a woman down at the emergency room is asking for her.

A tall woman? Adeline asks. With long gray hair?

Carl shakes his head. She's got a little boy.

Adeline puts out her cigarette. Lead the way, she says,
but she's already walking down the corridor ahead of Carl,
and his short legs can't keep pace with her long strides.

Adeline finds Lorna and Jimmy in the emergency room
waiting area. The boy is sitting on his mother's lap, leaning against her, his thumb in his mouth. He's looking about
warily, and when Adeline comes close he shuts his eyes and
burrows his head into his mother's bosom.

Yes, Adeline says to Lorna. What is it? Who are you?

George Blackledge said I should find you—

And at this Adeline must sit down, herself. Is it
Mrs. Blackledge? she asks. Has something happened to
Margaret Blackledge?

Lorna's story rushes out of her but it's barely a story
at all. It's more like a child's recitation of an incompletely
memorized poem, the words and images neither connect-
ing nor cohering.

Gradually, however, a receptive listener, one who isn't
intent on trying to winnow truth from falsehood or fact
from interpretation, hears an account of what has happened
out at the Weboy place, confused and disjointed though that
account may be.

She'd decided to leave her husband so Mr. Blackledge . . .
Donnie . . . she's married to Donnie Weboy? She and her
son lived at the Weboy place . . . but he's not a Weboy,
Jimmy, he's a Blackledge . . . and his grandfather came to
take her back to Dalton, North Dakota . . . and somehow a
fire started . . . at the Weboys' . . . a fire . . . in the house . . .
she doesn't know . . . maybe . . . somebody shot a gun . . .
maybe . . . but Mr. Blackledge said come here.

So I came, Lorna says and only now seems to draw a
breath.

And in that abrupt silence, the listeners—Adeline Witt
and Carl Skeller and Doris Rollag, another night nurse—
finally hear what needs to be heard: *a fire at the Weboys!*

Calls are immediately made, sleepers awakened, alarms
sounded . . . but by then none of the night's events could be
altered any more than the approaching dawn can be hurried or delayed by a single minute.

42.

<small>MARGARET BLACKLEDGE IS WAITING ...</small>

She and Alton Dragswolf agreed they'd leave the valley together, the path being too steep, rocky, and rutted for a climber to navigate safely alone.

Once they reached the top, however, Alton Dragswolf returned to his shack and left Margaret to try to hitch a ride into Gladstone alone, a driver being more likely to stop for a solitary woman than for two hitchhikers, especially when one of them is an Indian.

And alongside the road is where Margaret waits now, dressed in her mackinaw and dungarees, her cut and bruised feet jammed into her boots, and another pair of boots—George's—slung on a string around her neck like a yoke she must carry through this life. The fog that clung close to the valley floor has thinned to nothing but mist at this height and because of the highway's light-colored concrete and broken yellow center line, Margaret can see down the road for a ways in both directions. To either side of the road, however, darkness has claimed the distances for its own, and this country that so often seems to promise walkers or riders that they can travel as far and as freely as they wish is now as blank and uninviting as a wall or a precipice.

At least ten minutes pass before a car comes along and it does not slow. As it rushes past, droplets of mist rise and swirl in the air like snowflakes. The next car is traveling in the wrong direction but when its headlights find Margaret waving her arms the driver eases off the accelerator . . . but only for an instant and then the car resumes its speed.

The temptation to start walking in the direction of Gladstone is strong—George is out there, somewhere, the agent or victim of who knows what acts?—but Alton has assured her that eventually someone will come along, someone whose sense of mercy or, hell, maybe curiosity will not allow him to pass a woman standing alone out on the prairie in the middle of the night. An old woman. Alton didn't say the word, but he didn't need to.

Then an old Ford truck pulling a horse trailer drives past her, but fifty yards ahead its brake lights blink. The driver makes no attempt to pull over to the side of the road but is obviously waiting for Margaret.

She runs down the highway and when she's almost at the truck, its passenger door pops open. She climbs in, and as she does she hears the horse behind her, its stamping hooves echoing inside the trailer as if the creature would prefer to keep traveling.

Run into some trouble out here, did you? asks the young cowboy behind the wheel. He's wearing a sweat-stained hat but his torso is bare.

Are you going to Gladstone?

I ain't. But I can. He scratches his stomach as if that's an explanation for being shirtless.

My husband's there. He's hurt.

You don't say. The cowboy's drunk. He's still leaning

toward the passenger side and when he tries to sit up straighter he goes too far the other way. The truck's interior has the smoky-sweet smell of whiskey breath and cigarettes hand-rolled from pipe tobacco. One of those droops from the cowboy's lips. But you, he says to Margaret, you ain't. Just nervous, are you? Shook up?

I need to get to Gladstone.

The brim of his hat has been pulled low as if the young man needed to keep his identity secret. He pushes it back now and says, Gladstone it is. He tosses his cigarette out the window.

But the truck doesn't move. Having unexpectedly stopped in the middle of the highway, the cowboy can't seem to find the sequence of actions necessary to resume his journey.

Then let's get rolling, says Margaret.

Her command works. He muscles the truck into gear, lets out the clutch smoothly, and they're on their way.

He has some difficulty remaining in his own lane but Margaret remains quiet until his front tires touch the gravel shoulder and he jerks too hard, bringing the truck back on course.

Easy, she says. You're going to make me and your horse sick. You don't want that.

He grips the steering wheel tighter and leans forward and does a better job of aiming truck and trailer.

You ain't asked me where I'm headed, he says.

I know. Not to Gladstone.

Wyoming. My buddy Petey French is working on a ranch out there and he says he can get me hired on.

A man with his own horse and a willingness to work can generally do all right for himself in this part of the world.

Me and my old man had words, the young cowboy says.

Did you. Margaret gestures to keep him from drifting over the center line and he takes the correction nicely.

He don't want to give me my due. So I finally had enough of his bullshit and told him to go to hell and walked off. He knew if he let me go I'd be gone for good but did he give a damn? He did not.

Your story, says Margaret, almost reaching for the steering wheel but then relaxing back into her seat, reminds me of my husband's. He had a falling out with his father. And it came to more than words. Before George walked away, he knocked his father to the ground.

Good for him, I say. A man's got his pride. Don't tell me I didn't want to do the same. But if I had I'd be watching for the goddamn law every step. This way I'm getting away clean. No looking back.

Did you leave tonight?

This morning, the cowboy says and flashes a quick smile in Margaret's direction. I sort of made a few stops before I got up a head of steam.

And you're trying to make it to Wyoming by . . . when?

I'll get there when I get there. Right now I'm just feeling good being out from under.

The truck veers dangerously close to the center line and this time Margaret limits her correction to a hand signal, five fingers thrust straight out. The cowboy steers them gently back into their lane.

Are you from around here? Margaret asks.

My folks' place is just outside Wibaux.

Margaret sinks back into her seat again. I know where Wibaux is.

Me too. Behind me. And that's where it's going to stay.

She leans forward and peers through the windshield as though she's trying to see beyond the reach of the head-lights. I had a boy not much older than you.

The young man hazards a glance in Margaret's direction. Had, you say?

Thrown from a horse. Broke his neck.

The hell. New to the saddle, was he?

He could stay on a horse. And he could keep his shirt on.

The cowboy claps his hand on his bare chest. Ooh! You got me!

And as long as I'm talking to you like your mother . . . that home you're putting behind you? You just might want to go back someday. No matter how far you go.

Is that your boy's story?

The intervening silence lasts so long the cowboy could be forgiven for thinking that Margaret hasn't heard him. Then, with the lights of Gladstone finally in view, she says, James? No, James always stayed close . . .

Apart from the directions Margaret provides once they enter the city limits, neither she nor the young cowboy says much more. When the truck and trailer stop in front of Homer and Adeline Witt's house, Margaret thanks the young cowboy and quickly climbs out of the truck with her husband's boots in hand. When her door slams, the horse nickers a quiet question: *Are we there?*

But Margaret doesn't walk away, not immediately. She

leans back in the open window to ask the young cowboy a question. You know where Dalton, North Dakota, is?

Yes, ma'am.

You ever find yourself in Dalton, you look the Blackledges up in the phone book and give us a call. I have some shirts I believe will fit you.

43.

AFTER THE CALL ABOUT THE FIRE AT THE WEBOY PLACE wakens him, Sheriff Munson dresses and drives out to the ranch. When he arrives, the rural fire department is already there, though it's too late for them to do anything but shake their heads at the devastation and make sure no sparks have found their way to the barn.

Anybody make it out of there? Sheriff Munson asks one of the volunteer firemen.

Just the young gal back in town.

Did Blanche . . . , the sheriff says but then stops short of the question to which he has already been given the answer.

He walks back to his car and uses his two-way radio to contact the deputy on duty at the jail. Go on over to the hospital, Sheriff Munson tells Clark Rohr. Hand over the news. It's every last one of them.

. . .

Margaret's hammering on the Witts' front door brings Homer on the run, and when he opens the door and sees her standing there with her husband's boots held close to her chest, he says, You'll want to talk to Adeline.

For the second time inside an hour, Margaret Blackledge climbs into a truck, this time with Homer Witt at the wheel. During the ride to the hospital, Homer says not a word to her, and she soon stops asking him questions. When a man in this part of the world finds a reason to tuck himself inside a silence, nothing is likely to coax him out until he's good and ready.

The Hudson! It's here! Parked in the hospital lot in a neat row with the other dusty cars that delivered their owners here in the middle of the night. Homer has barely stopped the truck when Margaret jumps out and heads for the hospital's well-lit entrance.

As if the darkened corridors are marked with special directions for her to follow, Margaret Blackledge proceeds unerringly to the room where Adeline must be. Outside the door she hears the murmur of many voices, triply hushed by the hour, the place, and the occasion. And when she enters, even the murmuring stops. There are faces here she doesn't recognize—Nurse Rollag's, Carl Skeller's, the doctor's—as well as those familiar to Margaret—Lorna's, Jimmy's—but it is Adeline Witt's eye that Margaret seeks. There will be time, too much time, really, for the explanation of all that has happened outside of Margaret's ken, but for now Adeline merely shakes her head.

It's enough. For the moment, it's enough, and Margaret gasps as if someone had laid an icy hand on her bare flesh.

Although no commands to move have been given, the people in the room reposition themselves in a series of intricate steps that allows the two tall women to stand alone in their midst and for Adeline to convey to Margaret

Blackledge precisely the same message that the nurse delivered to Lorna within the hour: your husband has perished in the fire that burned the Weboy house to the ground.

Those who know Margaret Blackledge know that when her head nods at Mrs. Witt's words, it's due to her affliction. It's not, as a stranger might believe, that she is nodding in assent—yes, yes, I knew where George was going—or in acquiescence to the inevitable—yes, yes, autumn will end and winter will follow, yes, yes, there's nothing to be done . . . But of what she whispers there is no question. Oh, George. For me? For me, George? Then, as if by instinct, Margaret reaches for her grandson.

He leans eagerly into her embrace. Margaret walks a few paces off with her back to the small congregation, bouncing Jimmy in her arms all the while. She is carrying his thirty pounds, yet it is this little boy who has the real burden. He must now rescue two women from grief.

. . .

The next day Homer Witt learns from a friend at the fire department that Sheriff Munson plans to conduct an investigation at the Weboy ranch. Homer drives out to the site himself and arrives just as Sheriff Munson is about to walk through the charred wreckage. Though there is so little house left even a good memory would have trouble putting it back together, the sheriff still enters where the front door once was. Much of his inspection will have to take place in the cellar of the Weboy house since everything aboveground burned and then fell into the hole dug for the foundation.

The sheriff asks, Come out here to help me, did you, Homer?

Just spectating. You know us old firehouse dogs can't stay away from the smell of smoke.

Within minutes it becomes apparent the sheriff has lost whatever enthusiasm he might have had for this inquiry. Has he never before walked through a fire's ruins? Homer, of course, has had experience with conflagrations and their aftermath. He can see, as any fireman could, that this was a fire that blazed fast and hot and either turned everything into its own fuel or twisted it into an unrecognizable shape in the attempt. But Homer Witt says nothing to help Sheriff Munson. Homer doesn't, for example, caution the sheriff about how only a foot away from ash as cold as snow there can be embers waiting for a little air to blaze up again. Neither does Homer advise the sheriff that when he's kicking through the cinders and the fire-blackened lumps, he might have to rely on sound to tell him what an object is. Metal rings dully even through its layers of soot and ash. Porcelain thuds. Glass pings. Bone on a bed of ash makes no sound at all. And Homer keeps quiet about what firefighters do when they're in the presence of burned bodies. They smear Mentholatum under their noses as a defense against that odor that is a mix of sulfur, musk, seared meat, and melted copper, a smell that, once in your nostrils, will never leave.

The sheriff walks out of the ruins near where the back door was. His work is done, and why not? No matter what he might or might not find, the people who perished here won't be any less dead. Did the Weboys die in their beds? Since their beds have burned along with the floors they rested on, it can't be known. And even if he had cause to do so, Sheriff Munson has no desire to probe fire-withered corpses to see whether a charred skull or breastbone has a hole in it that could have been made by a .44 caliber bullet. Could the coroner discover something among the ashes? Perhaps, but Sheriff Munson won't call his colleague in on this one. Six people dead . . . why risk adding complication to heartbreak?

. . .

Arrangements are made. That is the phrase. In the wake of calamity arrangements are made, though everyone knows these will be for lives that do not want to be set in order or brought into line.

Adeline loans Lorna a dress and though the garment is too big in the shoulders and hangs far below her knees, it'll have to do until Lorna gets back to Dalton, where she and Margaret can try to put together a semblance of a wardrobe. For Jimmy there's nothing to be done but purchase new clothes at Sears.

Homer accepts Margaret's offer of George's boots. They're at least three sizes too large but they're good boots, better than Homer's, so he stuffs them with rags and wears them, adding a wobble to his bowlegged walk.

He's wearing those boots when he drives out to Alton Dragswolf's shack to retrieve George and Margaret's suitcases and a few of the supplies that had been unloaded from the Hudson. The food Alton is welcome to, payment for his hospitality and the loss of the revolver that George carried off. Homer doesn't bring George's hat back, because Alton hid it. He's already made it his own and he's been wearing it every day, peering out from its wide brim as he watches the edge of the butte for the Hudson to appear and once again make its careful way down the trail to his home.

The coffin that will be shipped back to Dalton is plainly too short for a man of George Blackledge's height, but that's a matter that will pass without remark. No one wants to risk hearing mortician Dugan's explanation that its length will suffice for what's left to be buried.

44.

WHILE THE FINAL PROVISIONS ARE MADE FOR THIS LIFE unforeseen, Margaret, Lorna, and Jimmy stay at the Witts'. Lorna and her son are given the spare bedroom and Margaret sleeps on the davenport. It's only two nights but they are nights to be added to Margaret's count of those spent in a bed not her own.

At two thirty in the morning of the day they are to depart, Jimmy wakes crying, and this is not a child's sleepy whimper but a full-throated, terrified wail. A closet door has been left ajar in the room where he and his mother have been sleeping, and Jimmy points to the closet's interior— a deeper darkness in the room's dark.

Jimmy's mother is right next to him but she's slow to rouse to her son's distress. She's confused, as sleepers sometimes are when they wake in strange surroundings. She looks in the wrong direction, toward the bedroom door and not toward her crying child.

By the time Lorna orients herself and turns to Jimmy to comfort him, the silhouettes of two tall women are framed in the doorway.

Once his eyes adjust to the dark and he's able to see what's there—or what isn't—Jimmy quiets.

Ssh, his mother says. Ssh. It's all right.

Lorna turns to Adeline and Margaret and offers them the same reassurance. It's all right, she says. He had a bad dream. It's all right. I have him.

. . .

The two women don't return to their beds but go to the kitchen. They sit in the dark and Adeline lights a cigarette from the open pack left on the table.

Did he have nightmares before? asks Adeline.

A few nights back in his own bed and he'll be fine, Margaret says. He needs to eat healthy and get some exercise and he'll be fine.

Well. Don't you be the one chasing after him. Let his mother do that with her young legs.

Margaret laughs softly. Lorna? I'm betting she won't last a year. The first good-looking fellow passes through Dalton she'll be flagging him down in the street, begging him to take her away. As long as it's to someplace bigger than Dalton.

And leave her child behind?

That's my guess.

Adeline shakes her head. That'll make you mother and grandmother both to the boy. You ready to take that on?

Just what George asked me. Yes. I'm ready.

The smoke that Adeline exhales shows up as a gray stream in the kitchen darkness. And what'll you tell the boy when he asks about his father and his grandfather?

I'll say they were good men. Good men who never wanted anything but what was best for him.

Adeline Witt nods and crushes out her cigarette in the ashtray.

Just so you know, Margaret says. That call I made earlier?

That was collect. So you don't have to worry about something mysterious showing up on your telephone bill.

Oh, hush. No one's worried about that. That was your daughter, I take it.

Margaret nods vigorously. That was Janie.

And how did that go?

She's not coming back.

Not even for—

She's not coming. Not that I believed for a minute she would. And she had a few choice words for me that I won't pass on.

Well, says Adeline, we raise them to live their own lives.

We do. We do indeed.

The women are silent for a long time and then Margaret stands up. I believe I'll head back to bed, she says. I'd like to get an early start in the morning and I imagine I'll have a hell of a time getting those two out of bed.

As Margaret walks past, Adeline reaches out an arm and pulls her close. Margaret bends over and rests her chin on top of Adeline's head. Margaret's vibration passes through her friend's skull and for an instant it's as if two women can think the same thoughts.

. . .

Jimmy Blackledge sits up high in the backseat on the suitcase still packed tight with the clothing that would have kept his grandfather warm during the winter to come. In the front seat the two widows watch Montana diminish with each revolution of the Hudson's wheels.

Soon they are among the first rocky rifts and ginger-red eruptions of the Badlands. When the lacerations in the landscape deepen into gorges, Jimmy climbs down from his roost and settles on the floor below the backseat as though something in the land's shadows reminds him of the darkness he saw in the closet the night before. On the floor he remains, moving the pegs in and out of the holes of the cribbage board Homer Witt gave him to amuse himself on his trip.

Once Dalton looms close enough for its water tower to glint in the October sunlight, however, Jimmy climbs back up to his perch as if, like an animal, he can sense the nearness of home.

Thanks to Meredith Kessler, Sue Ostfield, Kate Strickland, Patrick Thomas, Allison Wigen, Will Wlizlo, and everyone at Milkweed for their efforts on this book's behalf. A special thanks to Daniel Slager for his care and insight. Our conversations have been invaluable.

I'm fortunate indeed to be working with PJ Mark, one of the finest agents in the business, and I thank him for his friendship and support.

And thanks as always to Susan Watson, to whom this novel is dedicated, for her belief in this book and its author. Without her faith, there'd be no book.

LARRY WATSON is the author of eight works of fiction, among them *Montana 1948* and *American Boy*. He is the recipient of the Milkweed National Fiction Prize, the Friends of American Writers Award, two fellowships from the National Endowment for the Arts, and many other prizes and awards. He teaches writing and literature at Marquette University, in Milwaukee, where he lives with his wife, Susan. For more, see Larry-Watson.com

Interior design by Connie Kuhnz
Typeset in Warnock Pro
by BookMobile Design and Digital Publisher Services